Special Delivery

"Come on," Tyler yelled, powering through the water with strong, sure strokes.

April tried to emulate him, but her arms and legs were too numb to respond to her frantic request for more speed. Even her lungs refused to work properly; all of her chest and diaphragm muscles were slowing down from the cold. She couldn't get enough air.

Gasping for breath, she miscalculated the position of her head in the water and sucked in a lungful of the salty brine. Coughing and choking, her lungs and nose burning, she moved erratically in the water. Then she went under the surface. Her eyes were wide open as the dark waves closed over her head.

Terror gave her a spurt of energy. She flailed at the water, now her enemy, but only managed to raise her head above the surface for a moment. Not even long enough for a gulp of life-sustaining air. She went back down. There was a ringing in her head; she couldn't think clearly. Maybe she should just breathe in the alien substance and go peacefully.

As she sank, stars of light began to appear around her. Very pretty, she thought absently, trying to catch one in her hand. But her arms and legs didn't work at all now. They floated lazily, aimlessly around her body. The only sensation left was the powerful, all-consuming urge to breathe.

As the stars disappeared one by one and a great heavy darkness descended, she suddenly felt strong arms encircle her. They carried her up, up until her head popped above the water. The cold air stung at her face as a river of water poured out of her mouth and nose.

"No," she sputtered and gurgled, "it was warmer down there."

Tyler's voice was grim in her ear, as his powerful arms towed her through the water. "You're confused, April. Hypothermia. Lack of oxygen. I've got you now. Relax."

He slid the strap of her now heavy shoulder bag off her shoulder. It must have filled with water when she'd pulled it under with her. Through a haze in front of her vision, she saw it sink into the sea. She tried to think. Something precious in there. Remembering, her kitten-weak arms struggled against him. "The blueprints! Got to save them. They're important."

"Not as important as you," he said fiercely. "Let them go."

What They Are Saying About

Special Delivery

Special Delivery was a book I truly enjoyed reading. It was funny, sweet, suspenseful and a lot of fun to read. Tyler and April were well matched, and the story just seemed to flow. If you are looking for a fun read with a lot of action, you will love Special Delivery by Linda Wallace.

—Dina Smitr
Romance Junkies
dinasmith@romancejunkies.com

Special Delivery moves along at a fast clip, just like the pace April sets on her bicycle courier route. The somewhat chaotic and spunky personality of April shines through in every scene. Tyler is very much her opposite, at least on the surface and in the goals he has set for himself as a responsible and dedicated developer. But this is a classic romantic tale of how opposites attract. I particularly enjoyed how the romantic tension between April and Tyler kept shifting but new revelations engage your interest time after time. The suspense of being thrown together into several life threatening situations was the perfect foil for them to overcome their seemingly irreconcilable differences. Still we wonder right to the very end if there will be a happy ending for Tyler and April. Ms Wallace's descriptions of the area made me feel as though I was right there in the back of the van or on a rugged coastal island. The dialogue was fresh, believable and drew me into the characters experiences. Touches of humor offset the tensions generated by danger and star crossed romance. I will watch for Ms Wallace in the future. Overall rating: 3 Hearts

—Patrice
The Romance Studio
http://theromancestudio.com

Wings

Special Delivery

Linda Wallace

A Wings ePress, Inc.

Contemporary Romance Novel

Wings ePress, Inc.

Edited by: Leslie Hodges
Copy Edited by: Karen Babcock
Senior Editor: Anita York
Executive Editor: Lorraine Stephens
Cover Artist: Richard Stroud

Wings ePress Books
http://www.wings-press.com

Copyright © 2005 by Linda Wallace
ISBN 1-59088-658-5

Published In the United States Of America

Wings ePress, Inc.
3000 N. Rock Road
Newton, KS 67114

Dedication

To my favorite romance reader,

my mother.

Prologue

A very ordinary-looking man sat behind the huge, elaborately inlaid desk. Only the feverish glitter behind the brown eyes hinted at the extremes of which he was capable.

Two men entered the room and hurried toward the desk. One was small and ferret-like with furry gray-brown eyebrows and close-cropped hair. He glanced furtively around the room, his gaze resting only for moments on the face behind the desk before darting away again.

The other man dwarfed his companion. He was almost as broad as he was tall and as heavily muscled as a bison. He plodded a half-step behind the smaller man, and his head, covered with thick dark curls that grew almost down to his brows, swayed slightly from side to side as he walked.

"So," said the man behind the desk in a calm, quiet voice that covered the menace underneath like a tree branch hiding a nest of yellow jackets, "how did it happen?"

The small man spoke rapidly, stumbling a little over the words. "It was the draftsman. He was rattled, he says, trying to beat the deadline. Then the courier came, in a hurry like they always is, and wanted the blueprints right away."

"Right away," the big man echoed, ponderously nodding his head.

"So, the draftsman, it's the new one, Jim Stolz, says he grabbed up the blueprints without really looking and handed 'em over to the courier. When he realized it was the wrong set, he tried to get 'em back, but it was too late—the messenger was already gone."

He paused and risked a glance at the inscrutable face across the desk. He shifted his weight restlessly from one foot to the other. "Some kind of dumb, huh?"

There was a long silence broken by a slow, rumbling chuckle from the big man. "Real dumb," he seconded. He opened his mouth to continue but was effectively hushed by a sharp jab to his midsection, expertly delivered by his skinny companion.

When the boss finally spoke, the men had to strain to hear. "Maybe dumb." He rubbed his thumb over the bridge of his nose. "Maybe not. I'll deal with that later. Right now we've got to get those blueprints back before Nielsen sees them."

He got up, planted his hands on the desk and leaned forward. "Go after that courier." He glanced at the clock on the office wall. "He can't have much of a head start. I got word of the mix-up just a few minutes ago, and if we're lucky, there'll be other deliveries before ours. Do whatever is necessary to recover the plans."

The big man's face sagged into a mask of concern. "But the courier's a girl," he protested, "just a little girl."

A flash of contempt burned in the boss's eyes, but his face didn't change, not by even a twitch, nor did he raise his voice when he repeated, "Whatever is necessary."

One

With one final, lung-wrenching heave, April Thompkins powered her battered, fixed-gear Cannondale over the crest of what had to be the steepest street in Seattle. The bitter taste of extreme exertion flooded her mouth. She was more than ready for the rush down the other side.

But she didn't get a chance to coast. The black van she had noticed pacing her in the left lane for the last block or so suddenly swerved in front of her bike. A burly arm shot out of the passenger window and clutched at her as the van zoomed down the street. Thick fingers bounced off her shoulder bag and skimmed her arm. The van cut her off and forced her directly into the path of a Metro bus just as it pulled away from the curb.

April gasped and lunged down hard on the pedals, her handlebar missing the bus by mere fractions of an inch as she whipped in front of the startled, gray-haired bus driver.

Spurts of adrenaline pumped through her body as she raced down the hill, leaving the bus and van behind in a splatter of mud thrown from her back wheel. In the tiny side-view mirror fixed to her helmet, she saw both bus and van drivers lift their arms at the same moment to shake their fists at her in perfect synchronization.

April sucked in a great gulp of air and let out a hoot of laughter. As though she were the one at fault. Few drivers ever extended any of the normal rules-of-the-road courtesies to bicycle messengers anyway, but what kind of sick mind would think it was funny to grab her? Was he trying to steal her shoulder bag or what?

She rotated her shoulders quickly to release tension. She didn't have time to speculate about weirdoes. She had work to do.

April ripped open her Velcro arm pouch to glance at the slip of paper with the address of her current delivery scribbled on it. It had to be on this block. Dashing away the rain that dripped from her helmet, she scanned the street numbers.

There. The tall, dark-blue building that loomed just ahead.

April hopped her bike up over the curb, unclipped her Shimano shoes from the pedals while she was still moving, leaped off the leather seat and dropped the Cannondale where she stopped. Triumphantly, she raised her arms high above her head and did a victory dance right there on the sidewalk, ignoring the covert stares of the few pedestrians braving the foul weather. Inches from instant death, and she had made it—still gloriously alive!

A brief frown flitted across April's face as the adrenaline dissipated and her thoughts returned to business. There was no nearby place to lock her bike and no time to search out a safe spot. She was going for a personal best. This was her forty-seventh delivery today. It was getting late in the afternoon, but she still had time to beat her all-time record of forty-nine.

Fifty deliveries! Her eyes lit up as she thought about the possibility. That would be the perfect cap to the day. She would be in the same league as the courier stars at XPress Messenger Systems.

And she could use the extra commissions. April stared down ruefully at her shredded kneepads. That last spill she had taken when she had unexpectedly met a motorcycle at the end of an ally had really done a number on them. She badly needed a new pair.

Resolutely, April snatched up her bike. She'd take it in with her. If she could just sneak past the security guard, she would be in and out of the building in a matter of minutes and on her way to delivery number forty-eight.

The door to the building opened automatically in front of her. *Great!* she thought. She didn't have to wrestle with the door while holding on to her bike. More good luck—there were two security guards, but they were engrossed in answering the questions of a flock of Japanese businessmen clutching electronic foreign language translators. The guards were turned away from her just enough so she could whip past them through the lobby and on to a long bank of elevators.

April sprinted toward an elevator door that was closing, karate-chopped it open, shoved her bike inside and leaped in after it. Fortunately, there was only one other occupant—a tall, lean, dark-haired man who started back as she burst into the elevator. He might report her to security, but she would be out of the building before they could do anything about it.

"Hi," April greeted him cheerfully, hoping to win him over with a little charm.

Of course, he didn't respond in kind. "Bicycles aren't allowed in the building," he said in a reproving tone.

He had a take-charge air about him, as though he expected people to pay attention when he cited rules and regs. It was a beautiful, rich, deep voice, really, one that would sound right at home narrating a PBS television special on the endangered species of the Amazon.

She grimaced. Too bad he was using it more like a reprimanding parent.

"I thought my bike might enjoy a little elevator ride," she responded flippantly and turned her back on him, determined to ignore him for the remainder of what she fervently hoped would be a very short ascent.

As she whirled away from him, she heard the long waterproof tube of blueprints that poked out of her shoulder bag soundly whack him across the face.

She looked over her shoulder to assess the damage. "Oh, rats! Oh, really, I'm so sorry. I didn't mean to hit you."

Mortified, April spun around toward the man to try to make amends, her jacket casting off a shower of water in the process. His once perfectly groomed hair was now all mussed. Charmingly boyish-looking dark locks spilled down across his forehead. His cheek was branded with a long, dull-red streak and beaded with rain droplets.

"Are you all right?" she inquired anxiously.

He didn't answer. Amazingly, though, he didn't look angry. In fact, he was actually grinning at her. True, it was a very condescending sort of grin, but all things considered, his face could have expressed a whole gamut of emotions that would have been a lot worse.

"Let me help," April said, as she whipped a cowboy-style bandanna out of her fanny pack. She stood on tiptoe to dry his face, but the man took one look at the red bandanna and her gauntlet glove with the fingers ripped out and shot out his arm in an instantaneous block worthy of a Sonics basketball champ. He gripped her arm tightly, holding her away from him, as she stared into his amused-looking dark eyes.

They remained frozen in that tableau for what seemed an eternity. All was silent except for the ping of the elevator counting the floors. His hand felt very large and alarmingly strong, and she could feel its heat even through the sleeve of her Gore-Tex jacket. April's heart skipped a couple of beats before she was able to step back.

"I think you've helped me more than enough for one day, thank you," he said as he ran both hands through his hair to smooth it back.

"Well, I really am sorry," April repeated lamely before she turned away. "I didn't mean to."

She could feel his eyes inspect her as she watched the floor indicators on the elevator panel light up as they ascended. She was acutely aware of the tire tracks and the little puddles of mud and water accumulating on the parquet floor as the elevator leisurely rose.

She hadn't failed to notice his impeccably tailored and pressed navy suit and pristine white shirt. On her own clothes she knew mud thrown from her back tire splattered her from her calves to her neck.

Oh, to hell with it. April squared her shoulders and stood as tall as her four feet, eleven and three quarter inches allowed. She didn't give two hoots if he didn't like the way she looked. A stuffy, buttoned-down kind of guy like he was probably never did anything more exciting than call his stockbroker. He'd never know the thrill of trusting his life to his own strength and wits to punch through a wall of blaring traffic and come out on the other side a winner.

Still, she'd be happy to be out of the building in a few more minutes. Something strange and disturbing had happened when he'd grabbed her arm. It was a confusing feeling she didn't understand or trust, and she was glad she wouldn't ever have to see him again.

When the elevator stopped at her floor, April gripped her bike and charged out the door before it had fully opened. As she paused to get her bearings, her fellow passenger strode past her at a speed that indicated he was just as anxious to get away from her as she was from him and disappeared through a double set of ornately inscribed glass doors at the end of the hall. *Nielsen Development Corp.* the letters read.

With a sinking feeling in the pit of her stomach, April looked again at the bit of paper she clutched in her hand, though she already knew what was written there. She groaned aloud and rolled her eyes. At least fifty floors in the building and hundreds of firms, and the man she had accidentally assaulted naturally had to go into the same office she was seeking for her delivery.

She wasted a few precious seconds before she started down the hall, hoping the man would disappear into some remote cubicle and not reappear until she had dropped off the architectural plans.

When April pushed the double doors open, the woman sitting behind a long, marble-paneled reception desk looked only slightly surprised to see a mud-spattered courier and bike. "May I help you?" she inquired politely.

Unlike many of the people she had to deal with, this employee was well schooled in the finer points of reception, April decided with approval as she reached back over her shoulder to pull out the plans and look at the package tag affixed to the tube.

Drat! This delivery required a personal signature by the recipient; the receptionist couldn't sign for it.

"I need to hand-deliver these blueprints to Mr. Nielsen, Tyler Nielsen," April told the receptionist.

"Wait just a moment, please. I'll check with him."

April looked around while the receptionist put through the call. It was one of those super-deluxe offices with huge abstract paintings on the walls and half a dozen strategically placed, elaborate floral displays. Except for the brilliantly colored birds of paradise and greenery, the color scheme was a sophisticated black, gray and cream with lush carpets, textured fabric-covered walls and leather couches and chairs grouped next to marble-topped tables. The Nielsen Corporation was clearly a big bucks operation.

"You may go through," the receptionist said. "Mr. Nielsen's office is the last one at the end of the hall." She gestured toward a corridor to the right of her desk.

April started to push her bike down the hall but stopped when the receptionist cleared her throat loudly. April looked at her inquiringly.

"You can leave the bike out here," the receptionist said.

April hesitated. Her uncertainty must have shown on her face because the receptionist continued in a reassuring voice, "I'll watch it for you."

April propped her bike against a leather chair and walked quickly down the hall. She hated to leave her precious baby anywhere unlocked. Somehow, she always felt naked without it.

A discreet little plaque read "Tyler Nielsen, President" on the office door at the end of the long corridor. April didn't bother to knock, since she knew the receptionist had already announced her. She walked in briskly, anxious to make the delivery and be on her way, but came to an abrupt stop when she saw an all-too-familiar navy suit behind the desk. An unreasonable urge to run away pulled at her so strongly she actually took a step backward.

The man looked up from the papers he had been studying and started back so violently when he saw April his chair rolled back a few feet. "You," he burst out.

Then he threw back his head and let out a full-throated, rollicking laugh. It was so infectious April almost joined in until he straightened up and crossed his forefingers in front of him as though he were warding off a vampire. "Back, back. Don't get too close," he said in mock horror.

"I have a delivery for you," April said stiffly.

He clapped his hand against his forehead and eyed the long tube April held. "Of course. The blueprints. I should've known. I'm afraid your charming, umh, I guess I could say 'demeanor' addled my wits."

"You need to sign for them."

"Sure. Hand them over. Carefully, please. I'll sign."

April pulled the tag from the package and walked over to the desk to give them both to him. He scribbled his signature on the little slip of paper without even looking at it, apparently preferring to watch her warily as though she were going to attack him at his first unguarded second.

With a momentary pang, April almost wished she could have met Tyler Nielsen under different circumstances. Of course, she didn't have the time or the inclination to date any man, but he really was exceptionally good-looking. He was too tall for her, well over six feet, but so well built even his stuffy businessman's suit couldn't hide the muscles. And he had such beautiful dark brown eyes wrapped with long, thick black lashes; the color reminded her of a luscious chocolate bar. Chocolate had always been her downfall.

The glint of humor lurking in his eyes would have been appealing, too, if she hadn't been the butt of his joke. Well, she didn't have time to stand around and let him laugh at her. This was the moment to inject a strong dose of assertiveness.

He had finished signing the tag but made no move to return it. Instead, he sat perfectly still while examining her with a bemused expression on his face.

April held out her hand. "The tag, please," she said brusquely.

The man must be deaf. He still didn't move. She couldn't keep the irritation out of her voice. "It's my receipt. I have to take it back to the dispatcher."

"So," he said lazily, conversationally, as though she had all day for chitchat, "why is a little slip of a thing like you working as a courier? It's a hard, dangerous job, isn't it?" He cocked a dark brow at her. "And I can see for myself that it's definitely dirty."

April rolled her eyes. He was actually grinning at her as though he though he'd said something witty. *This guy might be nice to look at, but he's a throwback to the dinosaur age.* Client or not, he didn't deserve professional courtesy.

She put her hands on her hips, puffed out what little chest she had and thrust her chin forward belligerently. "Look, I don't have time to stand around and discuss my career choice. I have more deliveries to make. Are you going to hand over that tag, or am I going to have to take it away from you?"

He paid about as much attention to her threat as if she were a yapping Pekinese. He obviously didn't realize just how serious she was, because he leaned back in his leather chair and tapped his chin speculatively with the tag. "Are you always so impatient?"

April gritted her teeth. She felt as though she might explode. "It goes with the territory. You pay me to be impatient so you'll get your deliveries on time. And now you're holding me up, so some other poor client isn't getting his money's worth."

He finally had the good grace to look contrite. He extended the tag. "You're right. Sorry. It was thoughtless of me. Thanks for the blueprints."

April snatched the tag, whirled around and raced out of the room. She burst into the reception area to retrieve her bike, ignoring the startled look on the secretary's face, then tore out of the building. She didn't understand why she was in such a state. She had encountered plenty of rude business people before him. Why did Tyler Nielsen disturb her so?

She was so upset she didn't notice the black van trailing her until it pulled up beside her at a red light. She stared at it suspiciously. Was it the same van? Two encounters in one day? It seemed an unlikely coincidence.

She had just decided to shoot down the side street to put some distance between her and the van when the passenger door opened with mind-numbing speed and force, crashing into her bike, hitting her helmet and knocking her to the pavement.

Before she had time to do anything but let out one puny little screech, a huge man lumbered out of the van and scooped her up. He carried her to the back of the truck where another man, skinny and mean looking, opened the rear doors.

"No, really, I'm all right," April protested. "You don't need to take me to the hospital or anything."

"You fool! What'd you hit her for?" screamed the skinny man. "Couldn't you see the blueprints was gone? She's already given 'em to Nielsen."

April struggled feebly, trying to get away from the big man. She felt woozy. The door must have hit her harder than she thought. "Blueprints? You wanted the blueprints?" she asked stupidly.

"You said we had to stop her. So I stopped her," the man holding April said sullenly.

The skinny man darted around the truck, retrieved April's Cannondale and heaved it in the back of the van.

"Hey! That's my bike. What do you think you're doing?"

It finally dawned on April that she was in real trouble. She managed to free one arm from her captor's grip. She swung awkwardly at the big man and hit him in the neck, but she might as well have hit a post for all the effect it had on him. He didn't even grunt.

The skinny man ignored her, too. He had stopped screaming, but now he somehow sounded even more menacing. "I meant stop her so we could talk to her, you idiot. Slip her a few bucks. Get her to take the right blueprints to Nielsen. Convince him she gave him some other company's specs by mistake and get 'em away from him. Give him the ones we want him to see."

April's vision was getting fuzzy and black around the edges. The darkness closed in to a tiny dot like a fadeout in a movie. She vaguely heard the mean-looking man's voice as though it were coming from far away before total oblivion enveloped her.

"You messed everything up," he snarled. "Now I don't know what we'll have to do with her."

~ * ~

Tyler shook his head in self-disgust the minute the courier blazed out of his office. What was the matter with him? He never engaged in meaningless banter. It was completely out of character.

But she was so cute. Like a little firecracker, all impulse and emotion, ready to flare up at the slightest spark. He hadn't been able to resist teasing her.

Still, she was the kind of woman he always carefully avoided. Women who stirred up that much excitement were the kind who could get you into real trouble.

No, Tyler knew exactly the kind of woman he wanted. Nancy Simmons, the paralegal on the fifth floor, was just right for him. Calm, levelheaded, serious. She would make a perfect wife and mother—supportive, nurturing and capable. He had been checking her out for several months now. It was time to settle down, and Nancy would make the perfect companion and helpmate.

He should go down right now and ask her out for dinner. Everything was prepared to launch the next phase of his timetable. He was right on schedule. His business was flourishing, and thirty-one was the right age to marry and start a family. He sighed. Why did it all suddenly seem so boring?

He rubbed his eyes. He tried to picture pleasant, perfectly dressed and coifed Nancy, but all he could see in his mind's eye was a fiery, freckle-faced, green-eyed little warrior all decked out in the weirdest going-to-battle costume he'd ever seen.

He wondered what color her hair was. He hadn't been able to see a single strand under her helmet.

Tyler shook his head again and crossed his arms over his chest. It was no use. He'd ask Nancy out tomorrow after he got over this inappropriate interest in a total stranger. And the best way to forget anything that bothered him was good, hard work.

Tyler turned to his desk and pulled the blueprints from the long tube. He smoothed them out and began to study them with total concentration. In just a few moments he began to frown. These weren't the figures he'd expected. There were many discrepancies from the original bid from Smith's Contracting, but the most glaring was way too few and too small rebars. Any building constructed from these plans would be dangerously unsafe. Anger furrowed Tyler's face as he leaped up from his chair. Something was drastically wrong with the blueprints.

Two

Tyler punched the button on his phone console to buzz his executive assistant. He'd talk to Smith himself and find out what the contractor thought he was doing. Nielsen Development would never have accepted a bid with such shoddy construction no matter what the cost savings. Tyler's company was known for the high quality of its projects. It was one of the things he was most proud of.

"Yes?" Rita answered immediately.

"Get Ron Smith of Smith Contracting on the line," Tyler barked. Then he paused. No, something was fishy, week-old fishy, and it stank to high heaven. Better to talk to the person who prepared the blueprints first, then go to the head of the company.

"Cancel that, Rita. I changed my mind. And if I have any more late appointments, cancel them, too. I'm leaving the office."

"Anything else?" Rita inquired.

Tyler rapidly planned his investigation. He should talk to the courier first. She might have information about the company and the blueprints that could prove useful. At the very least, she could tell him who had given them to her.

He'd try to intercept her at her next delivery. She'd said she still had more to make today. But what company did she work for? There'd been some kind of lettering on her jacket. Tyler grinned as he remembered. The logo was mostly obliterated by mud, but he was sure he remembered an "X."

"Rita, see if you can find a messenger service in the directory with an 'X' at the beginning of the name. Jot it down for me along with Smith's address and phone number. I'll pick it up on my way out."

He disconnected, stuffed the blueprints back in the packing tube and grabbed his Burberry from the coat rack on the way out of his office.

"I found it," Rita crowed triumphantly, waving a memo slip in the air, as he approached her desk.

Tyler flashed her a thumbs up sign before taking the paper. "You're a wonder. Never let me down yet."

Too impatient to wait for the elevator, Tyler sprinted down the stairs to the parking garage. He wasn't sure what was pushing him so hard, but he felt a strong sense of urgency.

He threw the blueprints and his raincoat in the back seat, gunned the motor of his silver Lexus and shot down the parking ramps to the street. He had just punched in the numbers on his cell phone to call XPress Messenger Systems when he saw her.

Tyler's heart thudded painfully in his chest. She was struggling with some huge lout in back of a van stopped in the middle of the street. Then, even more frighteningly, her slight body went as limp as a rag doll.

"Put her down," he shouted ineffectually and smashed his fist against the steering wheel.

Blocked in by other vehicles several car lengths behind the van, his inability to do anything to help sent him into a frenzy. He'd never wanted to punch anybody as badly as the hulking giant who now climbed awkwardly into the back of the van, still carrying the tiny courier. Tyler opened his car door, prepared to abandon the Lexus in traffic so he could run up to stop what couldn't be anything but an abduction.

The driver of the car immediately behind the van started to get out of his car, too, apparently to make inquiries, but another small man who seemed to be with the giant waved him away. The small man slammed the double rear doors of the van, climbed in the driver's side, then the truck sped away.

Now that the van was no longer blocking the street, traffic started to move again. Tyler jerked his door shut and began to maneuver from lane to lane to close the distance between his car and the van. He prayed he could get to the courier before those thugs harmed her.

They had only driven a few blocks when Tyler pulled along side the van. He could see the driver's profile clearly now, an evil-looking weasel of a man. Tyler didn't want to speculate too vividly on what his plans might be for the young woman in the back of the truck.

Tyler tapped the car horn and waved his arm at the driver to get his attention. The weasel jerked his head around to stare at Tyler then mouthed some words that, from the look on his face, were definitely hostile.

"Pull over, you punk," Tyler shouted.

In answer the van veered off with a sharp turn onto a side street.

Tyler couldn't make the turn in time to follow. Saying a few choice words, he circled several blocks before he caught sight of the van again. Determined not to lose them this time, he followed closely behind while he planned his next move.

Plan. That's the operative word. He had reacted with pure gut instinct when he had seen the courier in trouble, not at all like his usual careful, controlled self.

What was he doing racing along like a TV cop in a chase scene anyway? This situation clamored for a real cop. He shouldn't try to handle it alone. He might cause more harm than good. The last thing he wanted was for anything to hurt the vibrant woman who had so intrigued him.

Tyler had just reached for the cell phone to call the police, when the van pulled into an alley. Tyler followed, and the truck slowed to a stop. The driver got out and walked back toward the Lexus. Tyler forgot all about the phone, as the need to find out if the courier was all right overcame his better judgment. He itched to confront the thugs. He leaped out of his car and strode purposefully toward the van.

"What'd you think you're doing, buddy?" the driver snarled.

They were standing just at the back of the van. Tyler started to question him. He didn't hear anything, but some instinct made him turn his head. Too late. He caught a glimpse of a beefy upraised arm, then his head exploded in a burst of light and pain. He clutched at the van for support, but he felt himself falling, falling. His face smashed into the pavement. The sharp stink of motor oil filled his nostrils, then blackness descended like a coffin lid.

~ * ~

April heard a dreadful eerie moaning. *Goodness!* She was making that awful sound, like some kind of wretched wounded animal.

Memory came flooding back. The black van. The door hitting her. Fighting with a man.

No. Not a man—a giant! What had happened to her? Where was she?

Panic hit. April struggled to sit up. It was no use. She lay on her side, her hands and ankles tied together behind her back. Her head hurt. Her arms and legs hurt. Actually, everything hurt.

The floor bounced beneath her. She heard motor and traffic noises. Of course. She was in the van.

Only dim light filtered in. She couldn't see much from her vantage point, with her cheek lying on a carpet or mat on the van's floor, except for the vague silhouette of her bicycle spokes.

Some kind of large bag was draped over her shoulder. Even with her ankles tied together, she retained a little leverage with her legs.

Experimentally, she swung her feet to see if she could kick the bag away.

She was rewarded with a loud groan. April's heart seemed to leap into her throat. She shrieked and valiantly tried to squirm away.

"Cut it out!" a familiar male voice ground out. "We must be tied together. The rope goes across my throat. You're strangling me!"

Him! How was it possible? "What are you doing here?" she snapped.

He exhaled forcefully. She felt his warm breath on the back of her neck under her helmet. It tickled the roots of her hair and sent a tingle all down her spine.

"That strikes me as an extraordinarily stupid question under the circumstances." His voice dripped venom.

"Stupid! Well, that's certainly a prime example of a turkey calling the duck fowl. I'm not the only one trussed up like a chicken waiting for slaughter!" April shuddered. That brought up far too vivid an image. "Anyway, I still want to know. What are you doing here?"

"Trying to rescue you, like a fool!"

"Rescue me? I don't need rescuing! And certainly not by you. I'll get myself out of here on my own, thank you very much. And if you quit being so sarcastic, I might even take you along with me."

He snorted contemptuously. "That's likely. Especially with you shouting at the top of your lungs. Did you ever think, in your carefully constructed escape plan, it might help if those two thugs think we're still unconscious?"

She considered the wisdom of that idea and decided to lower her voice. It was actually kind of sweet that he wanted to rescue her even if she could take care of herself. And, she hated to admit it, but maybe the situation wasn't quite so scary with someone there with her.

After all, there were two kidnappers. It would be easier to overpower them with a sidekick. And it couldn't hurt if her sidekick was over six feet tall and had muscles like steel.

She could feel some of that steel now as Tyler shifted his position. A heavily muscled thigh slipped under her bent leg. The spicy, intoxicating scent of his aftershave enveloped her.

"Thank you for trying to help me," she said in a strangled voice. "It was very nice of you."

"No, it wasn't," he said morosely. "It was really dumb."

Stung, she lashed out. "Why did you butt in, then? And what were you even doing there, anyway?"

"I didn't mean it was dumb to try to help you." His voice was gentle now. It felt strange to have him so near and not be able to see him. You could tell a lot about a person's intentions by reading their body language. He moved again, jostling her uncomfortably. That kind of body language was no help. April wished the exasperating man would just lie still. The quarters were far too close for him to be wiggling around.

"It was the way I went about it," he continued. "Modern technology, the ubiquitous cell phone, right at my fingertips. And did I think to use it? No!" he burst out, obviously forgetting his own admonition to speak quietly.

Self-righteously, April whispered, "But you still haven't explained why you were there. How did you happen to see them kidnap me?"

"The blueprints. The specs are all wrong. I wanted to ask who had given them to you. I was tracking you down when I saw the men put you in the van."

"That makes sense. Before I passed out, I heard the men talking about two sets of blueprints. What do you think is going on?"

"I don't know yet, but I do know we have to get out of these ropes," he said grimly. "You're right about being trussed up like chickens. We're helpless like this."

"My hands are behind my back. Maybe I can find a knot in your rope I can untie."

She felt Tyler hitch himself even closer until he was curved along the whole length of her. The cadence of his breathing seemed to change. His voice deepened and became huskier. "I think any two people this close together need to be introduced. Perhaps you could tell me your name."

"It's April." Her voice came out in a silly squeak. If it went any higher, he'd think he was tied up with Minnie Mouse. She cleared her throat and, with considerable effort, brought her voice down an octave or so. "April Thompkins."

She strained against her bonds, reaching toward Tyler. She stretched her fingers as far as they would go and was rewarded by touching the fabric of his shirt. She could feel the washboard-hard muscles of his abdomen beneath the fine, soft cotton. She sucked in a quick breath and heard him do the same. She squeezed her eyes shut even though she couldn't see anything anyway. *Get a grip,* she silently scolded herself. Who knew how much more time they'd have to work on the knots before the kidnappers reached their destination? After all, it wasn't such an ordeal. He felt perfectly wonderful.

Patting his shirt in a widening arc, she felt the roughness of a rope.

"I've got it," she cried gleefully.

"You untied it already?" he asked, his voice full of hope.

"No," she had to admit. "I found the rope. Now I'll just follow it down..."

A raucous squawk split the relative silence of the van. Her nerves already at the breaking point, April screamed and jerked against their fetters.

"I never thought I was an Adonis, but I don't ever recall a lady making a sound quite like that just from touching me." The strain in Tyler's voice betrayed the effort the joke cost him. "What was that noise, anyway?"

Excitement filled April with new purpose. "My radio! Why didn't I think of it before? The men didn't take it away. It's still in its holster under my jacket. If I can just get to it, we can call for help!"

She struggled in earnest then. But it was no use. She couldn't depress the send button. The full horror of the situation billowed and ballooned until it filled April's mind. What were the men going to do to them? She began to sob and flailed wildly, purposelessly, against the ligatures.

"April, shh, it will be all right. Don't worry. We'll find another way." His voice pierced her hysteria. It calmed and soothed. She wondered guiltily how many times he had to repeat the words before she heard them.

She hadn't given him a thought when she lost control. She'd probably hurt him, jerking around like that. "I'm sorry," she snuffled. Disgusted that she couldn't even blow her nose, she rubbed her face against the carpet to wipe some of the wetness away. "I don't know what came over me." She laughed shakily. "I've always wanted to experience everything. I guess this could be considered the ultimate adventure."

"Is that why you're a courier, for the adventure?" he asked in a conversational, getting-to-know-you kind of voice. He was transparently trying to distract her to calm her down, but surprisingly, April didn't resent his efforts. In fact, she gratefully played along.

"Yes. I want to try lot of things before I settle on a career." She was inordinately proud of what many would consider a weird resume. "I've worked in the reptile house at the Woodland Park Zoo, and I helped exercise the thoroughbreds and mucked out stalls at Emerald Downs, and after that, just before I got the job with XPress Messenger Systems, I changed light bulbs at the top of the Space Needle. That's a year-round job, you know." She considered a moment. "I guess my favorite jobs are where you use your body."

Tyler hooted softly. "You didn't have to tell me that. You've given me some bruises worthy of a first-rate soccer kicker."

"I'm awfully sorry. I'm really ashamed of losing control like that. It's just frustrating to be so close to help and not be able to use it."

Tyler sighed and his breath tickled her ear. "No need to apologize, April. I feel the same way."

He sighed again, deeper this time, and shivers catapulted down her spine. "Besides, I can't help but think you wouldn't be in this situation if it wasn't for me."

"What do you mean?" April demanded indignantly. "They grabbed me first. It wasn't your fault."

"This is all about the blueprints. If you hadn't delivered them to me, you wouldn't be involved. And I should have stopped them from taking you. I acted like a fool, letting that thug sneak up on me. And I didn't even call the police when I had the chance. It's all my fault."

"It most certainly is not! It's my fault. They tried to grab the blueprints even before I got to your office. I should have known right then something was going on. And then the same van followed me when I left the building. If I hadn't been so, so... " But she didn't want him to know just how much meeting him had affected her. She had been completely distracted. "Well, I should have noticed."

"But I should have—"

"No! I should have... " Then the import of their words dawned on April. Their argument sounded utterly ridiculous. She giggled.

Tyler's body stiffened, then he relaxed and chuckled softly along with her. "You're right. It doesn't really matter who should have. We're both here now."

April stopped giggling at that gloomy pronouncement. The laughter had driven their troubles away for a few moments. It had felt so good to forget about the danger.

April shivered. It was getting colder. They had been riding for some time now, and she didn't know how long she had been unconscious. Few traffic sounds penetrated the van. They must have been out of the city for quite a while. Apprehensively, she wondered where they were going.

She shuddered, but this time it wasn't from the cold. She didn't want to think of their final destination. Better to get more information from Tyler.

"It is about the blueprints, isn't it? What are they for?"

"They're for the hotel in a resort complex I'm building on Whistler Mountain. It's my best project." She could hear the pride in his voice. "A beautiful location and a design worthy of the setting.

"So," April puzzled, "did these men want to steal the blueprints for a competitor? Or maybe for an organization that's opposed to developing the mountains? To stop you from building or at least slow you down?"

She felt him shake his head. "No," he said slowly. "I don't think so, though I don't have enough information at this point to be sure. Anything is possible. Remember, I told you the specs are wrong. They're from a subcontractor who's going to put up the basic structure for me. The plans you gave me don't match his original bid. If he uses these specifications, the building would be unsafe."

April gasped. "You mean unsafe as in the building might fall down? People could get hurt?"

"Right."

April nodded sagely. "I do remember now. Two sets of blueprints. They were talking about it, but my thinking was so fuzzy after the van door hit me."

"They hit you with the door?" He sounded outraged.

"Yes. But I remember the skinny one tell the big guy he shouldn't have hit me, because he wanted me to go back and give you the plans they really wanted you to see."

April chewed on her lip as she tried to figure it out. "But why did they kidnap you if they're trying to fool you? It doesn't make any sense."

"No, it doesn't. They might not have known who I am, or maybe they thought it was too late to save their scheming hides. Or maybe they just aren't very bright. That could work to our advantage."

April hoped it would work to their advantage very quickly because the van suddenly made a turn, then slowed to a stop. She heard another vehicle crunch through gravel and stop next to them. Her body tensed as she heard a door open at the front of the van, then the sound of footsteps.

"One of them must be driving my car," Tyler muttered.

"I'll kick them if they get close enough," April whispered.

"No! April, don't!" His voice held a note of desperation as he tried to persuade her to abort her plan. "You'll just make them angry. We can't overcome them or get away with our hands and feet tied. We have to wait until... "

April jumped as the back doors crashed open and interrupted him. No light came in. It was dark outside now.

"Well, well," said a raspy voice, "wide awake now, aren't you? And thick as thieves. But it won't do you no good, so you might as well forget any tricks you're thinking up. I'm going to put a stop to any more planning right now."

The man climbed into the van and leaned over the couple.

"Help!" April screamed as loud as she could. "Somebody, help us!"

The man guffawed. "There's nobody around here that's going to hear you."

April ineffectually jerked her head from side when the man touched her face. She could feel ropes of muscles in Tyler's arms and legs coil in readiness, but he couldn't help.

The man stuffed an evil-smelling rag in April's mouth and tied it tightly. The cord bit into the tender flesh at the corners of her mouth. She pushed her tongue against the cloth, fearful she would choke. Fear accelerated her breathing. She heard a rushing sound as she dragged air in through her nose.

Behind her she heard a muffled shout extinguished. The man must have gagged Tyler, too. Then the doors slammed shut.

Tears burned April's eyes as the van backed, turned and gained full speed again. She felt a hundred times more alone since she couldn't talk to Tyler. She realized how much his deep, soothing voice had comforted her now that it had been taken away. Even when they argued, it made her forget about the danger. Now she felt utterly abandoned.

Soon, the van slowed again. April listened hard, all her senses alert. She heard a faint murmur of voices that seemed to come from outside the vehicle. The van crept along, stopped, then crawled forward before coming to rest again, where the motor's hum also stopped.

Metal groaned and clanked. Water lapped. A mournful whistle hooted. Powerful engines sprang to life. The van was moving again, but the wheels weren't turning.

The ferry! They were on one of the many ferries that crisscrossed the waterways west of Seattle.

Hot tears trickled down April's cheek and moistened the musty rag smothering her cries. Hundreds of people surrounded them on the ferry, and she couldn't call to them for help.

Most of the people were on their way to the comfort of their homes. But for Tyler and her, it was a ferry bound for nowhere.

Three

Tyler listened to the throb of the engines for what seemed an eternity. Unbelievably, mercifully, April's slow regular breathing and relaxed body indicated she slept. He was glad. The rest would help her face whatever ordeal lay ahead, and there was no question they were going to need all the help they could get.

Unless, he worried, April's ability to sleep meant something more sinister. Could she be suffering from a concussion? Perhaps she might have slipped into a coma.

A spasm of fury and frustration washed over his body. Not that he could do a damn thing about it even if she was unconscious.

He raised his head as much as the rope that cut into his throat allowed and tried to assess April's condition. She looked incredibly frail with her body arched back into a bow by her bonds. She still wore her biking helmet. If she didn't have a concussion, the helmet was probably what had saved her. Her neck bent forward, exposing her delicate nape. A wave of tenderness engulfed him. He longed to kiss the perfect pure curve.

Tyler breathed as deep as he could with his mouth gagged. A little of the salty, cold tang of the brisk air off Puget Sound penetrated the stuffy box of their van prison. He let the air rush out with a deep sigh.

Somehow, he wasn't exactly sure how or when it had happened, he and April were bound together by more than just rope.

Responsibility for her safety weighed heavily upon him. Certainly, April wasn't an easy woman to protect. She went tilting after windmills with far more courage than sense. Still, he couldn't help but admire her bravery. He couldn't imagine many other women facing such an ordeal with so much spirit. How could he get her out of this mess?

Tyler tightened his muscles as though he could simply command his body to burst free of the fetters. He ground his teeth against the gag. This lack of control would surely drive him mad.

He willed himself calm. All he could do now was wait. When the opportunity presented itself, he would be ready.

~ * ~

April woke with a jolt. The ferry had stopped. Motors revved all around her. The vehicles must be getting ready to disembark. The van moved forward under its own power again and clattered over the gangplank. She wondered where they were now.

How could she possibly have slept? But she knew fear and exertion had exhausted her, and the movement of the ferry and the lullaby of the throbbing engines had tranquilized her just enough to let her drift off.

Was Tyler asleep? She stretched her fingers until she patted his shirt. He was still there, of course, and awake, too, because she felt his muscles tighten when she touched him. That was somehow reassuring.

They had ridden in the van for more than an hour after leaving Seattle, maybe two. That might mean they had boarded the ferry at Anacortes if they'd been traveling north. They could be at any of half a dozen islands in the San Juans or even Canada. She wasn't sure how long they had been on the ferry, thanks to her snooze. Traveling south, the only ferry she could think of went to Vashon Island or Southworth, but unless they'd been driving in circles, it wouldn't have taken so long to get to the terminal.

The van hit a series of rough spots in the road. April's shoulder repeatedly bounced against Tyler's hard chest. She heard his muffled groan. She wished she could tell him she was sorry—that she couldn't help it.

The van switched back sharply. It climbed steeply, and she was thrown more forcefully against Tyler. She heard the motor labor in protest against the ascent. They must be going up a mountain. The sharp scent of cedars and the earthy damp smell of moss and ferns flooded the van.

They were on a very poor road; it couldn't be much more than a track. The van swayed and dipped, and she and Tyler were tossed about like marionettes. Her bike slid back and a pedal banged against her helmet. Thank goodness for her trusty old brain bucket, she thought fervently.

Finally, the van rumbled and bumped to a stop. April tensed. *Now what?* Her heart was pounding so hard and fast it sounded like a snare drum in her ears.

She heard a second vehicle pull up. Doors opened and closed. Voices, footsteps. The back doors crashed open, and a brilliant light flashed on her face. She scrunched her eyes shut against the glare.

"Okay, Harmon, help me get 'em out of here."

The hated gag was unceremoniously yanked out of her mouth, taking a good portion of skin along with it from the feel of it. April gasped and licked her split lip. She cracked open one eye to peek at what was going on, only to see a huge knife blade descending. April's eyes flew open in spite of the light, and she shrieked so loudly it hurt her own ears.

She had the momentary satisfaction of seeing the knife jerked away as the skinny man jumped back. He laughed unpleasantly, seemingly embarrassed at having been startled, then the blade flashed again.

April's eyes bugged out, but he only cut the rope where it fastened Tyler and her together. She let out a sob of relief.

The two men carried Tyler to the van doors and dropped him on the ground, as if he had no more feeling than a bag of potatoes. They must have removed Tyler's gag, too, because April heard the whuff of forcefully discharged air when he hit the dirt.

Outraged at Tyler's treatment, April forgot all about her own fear. "Just wait until I get out of these ropes. Are you guys ever going to be sorry," she whispered.

"He's too heavy to carry to the cabin. Cut his legs loose, Harmon. Make 'em walk."

In an instant, everything changed. April heard scuffling, blows, a roar of curses, then the sound of running footsteps.

She tried desperately to edge to the doors of the van to see what was happening, but she only managed to move backward a few inches. She froze when a gunshot blasted her ears. Then she tried to scoot away to the front of the van even harder, when the skinny man leaped in the back, his face distorted by rage and the wavering flashlight into a snarling gargoyle.

April cringed as he leaned over her. He thrust the flashlight into his jacket pocket so that it pointed upward and illuminated the stained, cave-like surface above them. Fingers as cruel as talons dug into her armpits as he dragged her out of the van. The ropes pulled and bit at her wrists and ankles as she flopped and bumped across the floor.

At the doors he handed her over to the big man—hadn't the smaller one called him Harmon?—as though she were a sack of mail. Harmon slung her under one meaty arm, gripping her around the waist, while he used his free hand to play a flashlight beam over a dense growth of tall trees and underbrush. Her feet dangled above the ground, pulling the ropes attached to her wrists until she thought they would wrench her arms out of their sockets.

The skinny man also skimmed the dark forest with his flashlight, the two beams crisscrossing like searchlights at a gala movie premiere. He waved the knife in front of him. "Come on out, or we'll cut the little girl to pieces and feed 'em to the bears. You wouldn't want that on your conscience, would yuh?"

The knife had looked big in the van, but now, in April's eyes, it took on the proportions of a machete. She resolutely tore her gaze from its mesmerizing gleam and called out as loud as she could, "Don't do it, Tyler. Get away while you can."

Immediately, Harmon clapped his hand over her mouth, the metal flashlight clinking painfully against her teeth.

The skinny man advanced on April, pointing the knife at her menacingly. "Come on, Nielsen," he shouted toward the trees. "We don't have all night. Get out of them bushes."

"It's no good, Willis." Harmon shook his head mournfully. "He's halfway down the mountain by now. A big shot like him isn't going to risk his skin for some little nobody bike messenger."

A needle of doubt pricked at April. Did Tyler really think of her like that? She pushed the unworthy thought away. What did it matter? At least he was safe. She was glad. Now it was her turn to escape, and she would, too.

"Yeah?" Willis rasped. "Let's see what happens when we cut a few bits and pieces off Missy, here. She just might scream loud enough to pull him back."

"Or more than likely he might run faster the other way." The big man turned so his bulk was between April and the knife. "We don't need to hurt the girl, Willis."

While April sweated in a fever pitch of anticipation to see who would win the dispute, the bushes by the side of the road rustled, as though a large animal were pushing through them.

Two beams of light jerked in the direction of the sound, and Tyler sauntered calmly into the clearing. "That's right, Harmon. There'll be no cutting tonight," he said firmly.

"Tyler, no!" April shrieked. "Run, run! Get away! There's still time."

Harmon put her down and pulled a gun from the waistband of his trousers. A gun materialized in Willis's hand, too. Two guns and two flashlights were trained on Tyler.

April gasped. He looked awful. Of course, his once perfectly tailored suit was torn and stained, but his face seemed to have taken the brunt of the assault. Scratches and scrapes scored his cheeks and forehead, and a line of blood trickled from his nose and over his chin to splash in a widening pattern on his white shirtfront.

He smiled reassuringly at April. He stood there seemingly as serene as if he were at a social function, his eyes squinted against the powerful flashlight beams the only sign of anything unusual in his demeanor.

The two men approached Tyler warily. His hands were still tied behind his back. With a gun pointed at him from each side, the men walked Tyler over to where April lay on the ground.

Willis bent down and picked up the knife he had dropped when he had pulled his gun. With one quick stroke he severed the ropes that bound April's legs then tucked the knife into a sheath that hung from his belt. He grabbed her arm roughly and hauled her to her feet.

Stiff and cramped from the long confinement, April stumbled when she took her first few steps. For a moment she feared she wouldn't be able to walk at all, but she fought against the weakness. She'd be hanged before she'd let either of those nasty men carry her again.

Willis kept a tight grip on her arm and the gun pointed at her head as he marched her toward a tumbledown gray shack that seemed to crouch at the base of the giant Douglas firs that encircled it.

She could hear Tyler and Harmon following closely behind.

When they reached the building, Willis kicked the door open and shoved April inside. Harmon and Willis flashed their lights around the dusty, cobweb-festooned interior.

April caught glimpses of a dilapidated table and chairs, a wood-burning stove and an old-fashioned hand pump at a corroded metal sink as each was briefly illuminated. The smell of wood rot and decay, with a musty kicker of rodent litter, assaulted her nostrils.

"It looks just the same as the last time we had to hide out," Harmon said glumly.

"Yeah, but we're not going to be here as long this time." Willis waved the flashlight at a door on the far wall. "Put 'em in the other room. They'll be out of our way there."

Harmon started toward April. "We might as well untie them. That room's tight. They can't get away. And they got to be hungry. I'll give them some of the stuff we bought on the ferry."

"You'll *what*? After all the trouble they caused us? I'd as soon string both up by their thumbs as untie 'em. And that food's for us. Don't you give nobody nothing."

Harmon's big head drooped. He pulled at the mat of dark curls on his forehead and opened his mouth, but apparently he couldn't think of anything to say because he closed it again slowly.

Willis darted over to April and poked her hard in the ribs with the gun. "In there. Now!"

Head held high, April followed his instructions with as much dignity as she could muster. Tyler walked right beside her as though he wanted to reassure her. Willis slammed the door behind them. She had noticed a metal latch with a padlock high on the door. Now she heard it click shut.

April slumped back against the door with a sigh of relief, glad to be at least temporarily away from the men. She blinked her eyes, trying to adjust to the light. Pale rays of moonbeams slanting in from a tiny window high on one wall were the only source of illumination. Tyler's white shirt glowed dimly in the moonlight.

April straightened and took a step toward him. "Tyler, why did you come back? You shouldn't have paid any attention to what Willis said. You were free. Why didn't you just keep going?"

He moved nearer, too, so they were almost touching. A faint whiff of his spicy masculine scent wiped out the must and mildew of the room that closed in on them.

"Did you really think I'd go off and leave you to the tender mercies of those thugs?" He spoke softly, tenderly. His voice seemed to envelop and caress her. "I never intended to run away, even before Willis threatened you. When we leave here, we'll leave together."

His words warmed her, but they didn't make sense. "But why did you run? You escaped. You could've gone for help. You could have saved us."

Tyler turned away and began to pace the room. "And just how much of you do you think would have been left to save by the time I'd gotten back? In case you haven't noticed, that Willis character doesn't have a very forgiving nature. Who do you think he would have taken his frustration out on if I'd gotten away?"

April swallowed hard. She had a very clear picture of what Willis would have done if Tyler had escaped. "But what were you doing, then?" she puzzled, mystified.

"The resort plans. They were on the back seat of my car. I'll need them to prove what Smith is up to—some kind of physical evidence to show he intended to build below standard."

He walked back to April. She was not pleased to note that her heart seemed to beat faster the closer he came. "I ran away from the car," he continued, "then circled back while they were looking in the wrong direction. I hid the blueprints in the woods. They're safe now, and good old Willis and Harmon are none the wiser."

April heard the satisfaction in his voice. She was amazed that he was already contemplating some court case in the perhaps nonexistent future while all she could think of was how to get out of the cabin. "You mean you risked your life—and mine!— just to get the blueprints?"

His voice was hard. "Not just my life," his voice softened perceptibly, "or even yours. Don't you see? If he's conning me now, he must have done it before. Who knows how many unsafe buildings are standing in Seattle like so many time bombs waiting to go off? I need to find out what other projects he's worked on, so the structures can be checked. We're talking about hundreds, maybe thousands, of lives."

April slumped to the floor, ashamed of her own shortsightedness. "You're right. But how did you know the blueprints were still there? They've been driving your car."

Tyler sat down beside her and leaned his head against the wall. "I didn't. But neither Harmon nor Willis seem any too swift. If they didn't bother to search you and take your radio away, I thought there was a good chance they didn't look over my car any too carefully, either."

He shrugged his shoulders and rolled his head from side to side. Even in the dim moonlight April could see the grimace of pain he couldn't quite conceal. He might pretend indifference, but she knew the beating was taking its toll.

He straightened. "Obviously, it isn't going to do any good to have the blueprints, though, unless we get away. It's time to plan."

April hopped to her feet. "I know one way to start. Watch this."

She slid her bound hands back down over her hips, along the back of her thighs and calves, down to her ankles, then she skipped over her wrists. She stood up with her hands now in front of her. "Ta da," she said as she triumphantly wriggled her fingers.

Tyler grinned at her antics, his teeth flashing white in the moonlight. "So you're quite a contortionist, but how is that going to help?"

"Because your hands work better when they're in front of you, of course." She dropped to her knees next to Tyler. "Turn around. I'll bet I can have those ropes untied in two seconds."

Tyler obligingly turned his back to her and leaned forward against his bent knees. It took more than two seconds, but finally she felt the knots loosen. "I've almost got it. There!" One more pull, and the ropes fell to the floor.

Rubbing first one wrist then the other, Tyler got up and swiveled to face her. "Thanks. That's much better. It's great to actually have a little blood circulating in my hands again."

"Come on, you can untie me now," she said, lifting her hands to remind him her wrists were still bound.

He grasped her arm, helping her to her feet. But instead of going to work on the ropes, he reached toward her throat and unfastened the strap that held her bicycle helmet in place. Carefully, he lifted the helmet away from her head. When it was removed, she felt her hair explode into its usual nimbus of utterly uncontrollable wild curls. "You can't image how much I wanted to do that," Tyler whispered huskily. "I seem to have a great need to know the color of your hair."

April knew she should move away, but she felt frozen in place. "It's red," she said, her voice cracking. "I'm a carrot top."

He bent down and lifted her arms gently up over his head, so they encircled his neck, then pulled her to him, raising her to her tiptoes. She was crushed against the hard wall of his chest, and she could feel the powerful beating of his heart. Her own heart was drumming against her rib cage as though it were trying to escape her body.

Slipping his fingers through her riot of curls, Tyler cupped her skull with his large palm. "Copper. Even in the moonlight, it glows copper."

Using the purchase he held on her hair, he tipped her head back as he bent his own head down toward her. "It's beautiful. Just like all the rest of you."

April saw him slant his head for better access to her mouth, then she closed her eyes and reveled in the wonderful soft warmth when his lips met hers.

A dim warning bell clanged somewhere in the far recesses of April's mind. This wasn't the right man, and it certainly wasn't the right place and time for a romantic encounter, no matter how absolutely delicious it felt. She should pull away. She should tartly remind him they were prisoners, that they were supposed to be planning their escape, but all she could think of was the glorious sensation radiating from her mouth to every part of her body.

A loud thump and raised voices coming from the other room jarred her all too rudely back to reality. April jerked her head away from Tyler. He sighed deeply, and she thought she could hear the same longing she had felt.

But that was ridiculous. He was not the kind of man who could ever be seriously interested in her. Certainly under normal circumstances, she would be bored in two minutes with a stuffy old businessman. Hadn't she read somewhere how traumatic events often forged a temporary intimacy between the people involved? *Of course*, she thought with relief, *that's all that's going on here*. She needn't feel guilty or wonder about the intensity of her reaction to Tyler. It was simply a natural consequence of their being thrown together in a crisis situation.

Tyler must be thinking along the same lines, April reasoned, not bothering to analyze her vague sense of disappointment, because he lifted her arms from around his neck, pulled away and began, with renewed urgency, to work on the ropes.

The men's voices were loud enough to clearly discern between Harmon's guttural, slow speech and Willis's fast, higher-pitched shrill.

"Of all the partners I could of teamed up with, I had to pick the biggest idiot in the world," Willis whined. "First you hit the girl so we have to nab her, then you top that by whacking Nielsen."

"How was I supposed to know it was Nielsen?" Harmon protested.

At that, Tyler patted his pockets, apparently finding them empty. "They took the time to search me," he deduced grimly. "Got my wallet, ID, everything."

"I just can't think of a way out of this," Willis said, his voice more subdued now. April had to strain to hear. "If the girl had disappeared, we might've been okay, but not Nielsen. I knew we was done for the minute I saw his driver's license."

"Maybe Mr. Smith will be glad we got rid of Nielsen. His plan was messed up anyway. Now Nielsen can't go after him."

Tyler nodded as though Harmon's words confirmed his own thinking. "I knew Smith had to be the one behind all this. Those blueprints couldn't have originated from lower down the chain of command."

"There you go, spouting off like a moron again," Willis shouted. "Who was supposed to see to it that Nielsen didn't find out about the plan? The boss spent a bundle setting the whole thing up. Now it's all down the tubes. It don't matter that Stolz gave the blueprints to the courier. The boss is gonna blame us, too!"

"Good," Tyler said with macabre-sounding satisfaction, "those hoods are in trouble, too."

April couldn't understand why he sounded so pleased. Hadn't he heard all of those disturbing phrases like "the girl had disappeared" and "we got rid of Nielsen?" Who cared if Willis and Harmon were in trouble, when she and Tyler were in such a fix?

"Maybe it's time to move on again," Harmon said morosely. "I hear there's plenty going on in Tucson."

"Maybe you got a good idea for once in your life. Course we don't have much cash to make our move, but I know where we could turn that fancy car of Nielsen's over for some quick bucks. It might be enough to get us out of here."

"Let's sleep first; I'm tired."

"No! There's no time for sleeping unless you wanna do it six feet under. We should'a reported back to Smith hours ago. He's after us already."

"What about them in there?"

April held her breath.

"Leave 'em," Willis ground out. April breathed again. "I'd just as soon not have a murder rap if I don't have to. They might get away, but it'll take a long time—plenty of time for us to do what we need to. They've seen our faces, but we're on file with the Feds anyways, so it don't make much difference. And if they starve, who cares?"

I do, April thought, puffing up indignantly. Tyler grinned at her as though he could read her mind and put a cautionary finger to his lips. Then he went back to working on the knots at her wrists, and the bonds fell away at last.

"Thank goodness," April murmured. She slipped her gauntlet gloves off to rub away the numbness from the pressure of the bindings. The gloves had afforded her quite a bit of protection, but still her wrists ached. Tyler'd had nothing to protect him from the bite of the ropes. *How much pain had he endured?*

She could hear the men moving around in the other room. Harmon's heavy lumbering tread approached the door to the room she and Tyler were locked in. April pulled her radio from its holster, resolving to hit him over the head with it if he came through the door. They were too far away from the station now to contact the dispatcher for help, but she was sure it would make an excellent blunt instrument.

The padlock on the door rattled as though it had been given a hard jerk, then Harmon's footsteps moved away. April's tense muscles relaxed, and she lowered her weapon.

"I guess he was only checking to see if the padlock is secure," April said.

"A good thing, too," Tyler said, sounding exasperated. "Just how much of a dent do you think that puny little radio would have made on Harmon's thick head? Not to mention the fact you probably would have to pole vault to even reach it."

"Is that so?" April flared, putting her hands on her hips, stretching to her full almost five feet and glaring at him. "Would you rather I just stand around and wait for them to tie us up again?"

Tyler sighed. He seemed to be making quite a habit of it. "What I would rather you do is think before you take any action that could get you hurt."

April softened her stance a little. "I'm not going to get hurt, and I do think first, really I do." She paused to listen intently to sounds that were coming from outside the cabin before she continued. "They've gone outside now. If you boost me up, I think I can see out the window."

Tyler lifted her with ease, and she scrambled up to stand on his shoulders so she could peer out the tiny window. She used her jacket sleeve to wipe away the cobwebs and grime that shrouded the single small pane of glass.

"Good. I can see the van. They're packing up all right. It looks like they're getting ready to leave."

April stiffened then shook her fist vigorously at the window. "Hey! Watch how you handle my bike."

"Would you please hold still?" Tyler growled. "You don't need to do a war dance up there. You're supposed to just be observing."

"But Harmon threw my bike out of the van," April cried in protest. "It must have sailed a good twenty feet through the air, and it landed upside down in a big bush!"

"Hold still anyway. It won't help your bike to pile drive me through the floor. What are they doing now? I thought I heard an engine start."

"You did. Both of them. They're turning around. They're going down the mountain. Oh! Super! Tyler, you can put me down now. They're gone."

April slipped down to sit on Tyler's shoulders. He reached up to grasp her waist, bent his head and swung her down to the floor as easily as if she had been a child.

April turned to search his unfathomable dark eyes. They were all alone now.

Four

Tyler broke the long silence. "They could come back. We'd better get out of here now while we have the chance."

He spoke reluctantly, April thought, as though he might prefer to remain right where they were. Was he remembering what had happened just a few moments earlier? Why had he kissed her, anyway? What had he felt? What had he thought?

She hated to admit it, even to herself, but she knew exactly what she would like to do if they had the option, the leisure, to hang around for a few more hours.

Without conscious volition her hand strayed to her mouth, and she touched her lower lip with a forefinger. Remembered sensations of Tyler's passionate kiss flooded her nervous system. She dropped her hand as quickly as if she had been burned.

Tyler turned away from April slowly. Was it her imagination, or did he have to force himself to move away? Even if he didn't want to leave her, he apparently overcame his reluctance. Once he was facing away from her, he walked quickly to the padlocked door, put his shoulder against it and pushed. It didn't move.

Tyler grunted, adjusted his position and pushed harder. Nothing happened. He moved away, rubbed his shoulder and sighed in exasperation.

"As old as this building looks, you'd think it would just crumble away, but no such luck, naturally. I'll take a run at it and see if that works."

Tyler backed away from the door and bent over like a football tackle preparing for the charge. April slipped over to him and caught his arm.

"No, don't. You're already hurt. Banging into the door can only make your injuries worse."

Tyler brushed her hand away and bent deeper, an intent look on his face. "We have to get out of here, April. This is the only way."

April grimaced. *Why are men always so stubborn?* she wondered as she whipped in front of him to block his run. They never considered a woman might have an idea or two of her own.

"What about the window? It's small, but I think I might be able to get through it if you lift me up again."

Tyler straightened and turned to consider the window. He rubbed his jaw reflectively then shook his head. "I don't think so. Look how tiny it is. And you'd have to break it. The frame is fixed in the wall. It doesn't open."

"So? It can't be that hard to break a little pane of glass." April marched determinedly toward the wall. "I want to try it. It's a better option than throwing yourself against the door."

She slipped her backpack off and pulled her radio from its holster. She hefted it in the palm of her hand, testing it for weight, and looked at Tyler expectantly, as though he had already agreed to her plan.

He threw up his arms, apparently in defeat. "All right. But here, use this to protect yourself." He took his suit coat off and gave it to April. "Your radio might be hard enough to break glass, but wrap my coat around your hand and arm first."

April shook her head and handed the jacket back. "No. Pieces of broken glass might fall down on you. Cover your head with the coat."

Tyler folded his arms across his chest and glared at her. "Now look here, April, I'm not going to argue with you over every little thing. Either you use the coat or I won't lift you up."

"Men," April grumbled, but she took the coat.

Looking very satisfied with himself, Tyler boosted her up to the window as he had done before.

"Okay. Shut your eyes and duck your head. I'm ready," April cried.

She swung the two-way radio at the window as hard as she could, but it just bounced away harmlessly.

"Rats!" Disappointment instantly deflated her.

"Don't worry. That was just a warm-up. Try again." Tyler's voice sounded encouraging but muffled. She was probably squashing him.

April drew her arm back and, with a ferocious karate-style cry, smashed the radio against the window with all her strength. An explosive shatter of glass rewarded her efforts.

"I did it! It worked," she whooped.

Tyler's groan reminded her just exactly where she was bouncing in glee.

"Sorry," she said, instantly repentant. "Just let me clear away the rest of the glass, and I'll see if I can fit through."

April nudged the last few pieces of jagged glass from where they clung to the window frame and threw them outside. She hoped she wouldn't land on any of the razor-sharp splinters when she jumped to the ground.

She handed the radio and the suit jacket down to Tyler. "Be careful," he admonished, as she momentarily swayed on his shoulders before catching her balance. He sounded worried. He was probably convinced she would break her neck. Men like Tyler never thought a woman could do anything that might remotely be considered daring or even athletic. Despite all of his obvious muscles, she bet she could beat him in any number of physical contests.

"Piece of cake," was all she said, giving herself full credit for admirable self-restraint.

Carefully, she thrust her head out the window. The rush of pine-scented air almost made her dizzy. It smelled of freedom.

She twisted one shoulder through the tiny opening then snaked the other shoulder outside, too. Tyler no longer supported the bulk of her weight. He still grasped her ankles, but the window frame cut cruelly into her middle. She braced her palms against the rough boards outside the window, trying to ease some of her weight onto her arms.

It was a lot farther down to the ground than she had thought it would be. She probably should have worn her helmet to protect her head, but it was too late now; she didn't want to squeeze back through the window.

She wriggled and squirmed, but her hips stuck fast. "Oh," she moaned, "I always knew chocolate would be my undoing."

"What?" Tyler called.

"Never mind. Just push, Tyler. Push really hard."

Quarter inch by quarter inch she scraped her hips through the narrow aperture. She could feel her biking pants being pushed down toward her thighs and briefly considered imperiling her already precarious perch to give them a tug, but quite reasonably, she thought, she decided to hell with it; modesty really wasn't an issue under the circumstances.

Her skin felt like it was being shaved away, but by pulling with her arms and with Tyler pushing her legs, she made a little more progress. *I wonder if this is the way a baby feels on the way out of her mom*, she thought. Contracting the muscles in her buttocks to make them smaller, she gave one final heave with her quivering biceps, and her lower body slipped through the window. It really did feel like a second birth.

Whoosh! The ground came up to meet her with a terrific rush. April ducked her head and hit the ground in a tucked position.

Scrunched into a ball, she rolled down an incline for several yards before she gained enough control of her momentum to stop. Colliding with a large clump of salal bushes helped.

April unfolded her arms and legs and tried to sit up. Her chest felt peculiarly hollow. She gasped for air. The plunge down the hill had forcefully expelled every cubic inch of oxygen from her lungs.

"April! Are you all right? Where are you?" she heard Tyler call anxiously.

It took a couple of tries to get her voice to work, and it still came out as though she had inhaled from a helium balloon.

"I'm okay. I'll go around front and see if I can get the door unlocked."

Experimentally, she got up on one knee. Yup, the trees and the cabin were still spinning around her as though she were on a carousel, but at least the carnival ride seemed to be slowing down a bit.

She stood and brushed at the debris that clung to her clothes and hair. There were enough leaves and pine needles on her to mulch a garden. Her biking shorts were soaked through, too, from the wet grass and ferns, but at least it had stopped raining for now, and her waterproof jacket had protected her upper body from the damp.

She wobbled up to the front door. It sagged crookedly from one loose hinge where Willis had kicked it open. Entering the cabin and crossing the larger room quickly, she saw with relief a key sticking out of the bottom of the padlock that locked the door to the smaller room. She'd feared she would have as much trouble opening the door from this side as they'd had from the other. Thank goodness at least one thing was going to be easy.

"I'm here, Tyler. There's a key. I'll have you out in a second."

She unfastened the padlock and flung the door open. She had only left Tyler moments before, but she felt ridiculously glad to see him again. She threw her arms around him and hugged him as hard as she could, but when he subtly changed the embrace from the reunion of long-lost friends to something more sensual, she reluctantly pulled away.

Tyler cleared his throat, but his voice still sounded husky. "Let's see if we can find some kind of light."

April looked around the room. A window pierced each of the three outer walls, but they were only slightly larger than the one she had climbed through and were also positioned high near the roof joists. There was no ceiling, only open beams and a steeply pitched roof. More light than in the smaller room managed to penetrate the gloom, but April could still barely make out the shadowy outlines of the few pieces of furniture.

"Aha," Tyler said, moving toward the table, "it looks like Harmon and Willis left us a few of the amenities."

He picked up an old-fashioned glass kerosene lantern and squinted at it as he held it up toward one of the windows. "Still has fuel." He patted across the top of the table. "We're in luck. Matches, too."

He removed the cover of the lamp, struck a match and lit the wick. The odor of sulfur and burning kerosene filled the room. After carefully adjusting the flame, Tyler replaced the curved glass cover, and a mellow yellow glow cut through the darkness.

April felt dismay again at the sight of the damage done to his face. She swallowed a cry of distress, darted over to him and tugged at his sleeve. "We need to clean you up. Come on, let's see if we can get some water out of that rusty old pump."

Looking over her shoulder to make sure Tyler followed, April went to the sink and furiously pumped the handle up and down. A thin trickle of reddish-brown water flowed into the basin. April continued to pump until the water cleared a little then pulled out her bandanna. She took off her gauntlet gloves, laid them on the counter with the bandanna and picked up a wafer of dried-up, cracked soap that lay next to the base of the pump. She rinsed the soap off, washed her hands, then wet the cloth and lathered it up. Tyler stood patiently while she soaked the crusted blood and wiped it away as gently as she could.

Was it really only a few hours ago when he had jerked away from the very same bandanna when she had tried to mop the raindrops from his face in the elevator? It seemed a millennium away.

Tyler winced when she cleaned a particularly deep cut. She tried to reassure him. "Sorry. I'm almost finished. It won't be much longer."

She rinsed and rung out the bandanna then squinted up at his face to evaluate his injuries. "We really need some kind of disinfectant. I used to carry a mini first-aid kit, but I got rid of it to lighten my load. Every ounce makes a difference in speed, you know."

Tyler groaned. "No, I didn't know, but I'm glad, if it means you don't have any Mercurochrome. My grandmother used to put it on every little scratch, and it burned like the devil."

"You won't be glad if you get an infection. You have to take care of cuts like this," she lectured sternly as she dabbed at his face.

It was a handsome face in spite of the bruises and scrapes—a truly sublime example of masculine beauty. It had been better when she'd been concentrating on the job she was doing; now that she was almost finished, the face she'd been working on came into sharper focus. April's fingers trembled slightly as she stroked along the hollow, rough plane of his cheek.

His forehead was broad with heavy dark brows set far apart and shadowing those luscious chocolate brown eyes. His nose was a bit too prominent, but on Tyler it merely looked proud. His chin was square, strong and angular. His lips were a trifle thin, but his mouth was wide, and when he smiled his wonderful generous smile, he displayed perfect, brilliantly white teeth.

A dark, heavy beard was beginning to shadow his cheeks and chin, and when April's fingertips grazed the sandpaper roughness, the trembling became more noticeable. *Steady*, she thought, *as much fun as it might be, this isn't the time to ravish him.*

She stepped away from him. She'd cleaned his wounds as thoroughly as she could; she had no excuse to continue caressing his face.

Then she noticed he was staring at her with as much concentration as she had exerted when she had been examining him. Self-consciously, she ran her fingers through her tangled damp curls and dropped her gaze to the floor. She must look a fright.

"I was just wondering if you like mountain climbing," he said with a strange intensity.

Surprised, it took her a minute to frame a response. "Why, I don't know. I haven't tried it—not the real thing with ice axes and crampons and all—though I like hiking and mountain biking."

She thought about it some more. He waited quietly, looking tense and expectant, as though he really wanted a serious answer.

"I suppose I probably would. I used to love the sense of space and to look at the city when I was up on the Space Needle, changing the light bulbs. And if you were in the mountains, the views would be spectacular, and the air would be great."

Warming to the subject, she continued with more enthusiasm, emphasizing the points she made with wide arm gestures. "Then there's the challenge. Think how super it would feel when you finally made it to the top. Just you against the mountain, and you won!"

She paused, wondering why he had asked her such an off-the-wall question in the first place.

"So, do you climb?"

"No," he answered dully.

She waited for him to continue, but instead, he took the bandanna from her hand, rinsed it and began to clean her face. It was filthy, she supposed. She probably shouldn't let him use the cloth on her, since it had been in contact with his blood and what with AIDS and

Hepatitis C and all, but then, he had rinsed it thoroughly, plus she had already gotten his blood on her hands. She'd never given a thought to the possibility of disease when she'd seen he'd needed attention.

When it became clear he wasn't going to pursue the subject of mountain climbing, April prodded, mumbling through a faceful of wet cotton. "If you don't climb, why did you ask me about it? We're going down a mountain here to get home; we don't have to climb one."

Tyler removed the damp cloth and stepped back to scrutinize her face as though he were an artist studying the last few brush stokes of a painting. He came closer, pulled a twig from her hair and rubbed her chin with his thumb, but still he didn't answer.

April was practically jiggling in place with impatience. Finally, exasperated, she burst out, "Well? What's mountain climbing got to do with anything?"

Seemingly satisfied with his clean-up job, Tyler rinsed the bandanna one last time with irritating slowness and draped it over the sink to dry. "My parents would have loved you," he said in a tight voice.

April rolled her eyes at the non sequitur. The blows to his head must have affected his brain more than she thought. But, curious about what was on his mind, she followed his cue. "Why would they like me?"

"Would have. They're dead," he said curtly.

"Oh, Tyler, I'm so sorry."

In a flash April envisioned her own parents—her dad with his big woolly beard, a faded flannel shirt buttoned over his comfortable pot belly; her mom, petite with bright red hair and lots of energy like April, only now in middle-age beginning to get a little plump—sitting around the long dining room table drinking coffee and listening patiently while April spilled out all her dreams and goals. Even as an adult, she realized how much she relied on knowing they were always there for her. How awful it would be not to have that solid underpinning of love and support.

Impulsively, April reached out to comfort Tyler, but he shook her hand away. "Don't, April. It happened a long time ago. I was eight. I certainly ought to be over their death by now."

"Eight! You were just a little boy, practically a baby. What happened to them? What happened to you? Who took care of you?"

"The same grandmother who wielded the Mercurochrome wand." He grinned crookedly, but April thought a certain grimness underscored the humor. "She had a cure for everything. Mustard plasters for a stuffy nose—yes, they do really exist—a mouthful of soap if you said a bad word, and a tonic of molasses and garlic every spring and fall whether you needed it or not."

April had a sudden startlingly clear vision of his childhood. "Oh," was all she could think of to say.

"They died in a climbing accident. Scaling Mount Rainier. The Emmons Glacier." His words shot from his mouth in short, hard bursts like bullets from a revolver. "It should have been an easy exercise for them. They'd been on a lot harder climbs, even the Himalayas. But they left me in the tent with one of their climbing buddies and just never came back."

"You were there! With them?"

"Sure. I always went along. No schedule was my schedule when I was little. I'd never been to school before Grandmother took over."

He laughed harshly, self-deprecatingly. "Of course, I thought it was great when I was little, when we were ricocheting all over the globe. What kid wouldn't? It was like being Tarzan and Sky King and Wild Bill Hickock all rolled into one."

He paused, closed his eyes and passed a hand over his brow before he continued. "When I grew up, I began to see things differently."

"How?" April asked, though she wasn't sure she really wanted an answer, because now he was staring at her in an accusatory manner, though what she had to do with it she couldn't imagine. "Before your parents died, it sounds like you had a wonderful time."

His lips curled into a mocking grin. "I thought you'd see it that way. You remind me of my parents, especially of my mother, though you don't look anything like her. She had long dark hair and was tall and beautiful."

Well, thanks a whole bunch, April thought, as she straightened her spine and tried to stretch a little higher.

"They were selfish and irresponsible," he said harshly. "They never gave a thought to how their silly adventures might affect anyone else. Grandmother told me how she suffered every time we were off on some wild escapade."

"But they lived out their life the way they wanted. They didn't bend to somebody else's rules."

He glared at her, condemnation plain in his eyes. "What about your parents? How do you think they feel about you hotrodding around Seattle on a flimsy bike? Or risking your neck on top of the Space Needle?"

"My parents? Me?" she stammered. Stricken, she considered what he had said. Her parents had affectionately called her their little tomboy when she had raced her tricycle all over the neighborhood and competed with bigger boys to see who could climb the tallest trees. She was the youngest of her parent's brood of children, but she had always been able to keep up with her older brothers and sisters.

She chewed on her lip as she reviewed her past from a different perspective. Had her parents worried about her? Did they now?

Funny, but she'd never really thought about it before, maybe because their acceptance of her seemed so complete. Perhaps they did worry. It wasn't unreasonable to think they might, but they never condemned her for her choices or tried to talk her out of her plans. They never tried to change her.

"My parents love me," April said slowly, still thinking about how they must feel. "So even if they do worry, it's more important to them for me to be happy. To live the way I want to."

Tyler shook his head, looking grim. "So you think. Ask them how they feel when they're looking down at you in your coffin. Because that's what happens, you know. One way or another, thrill seekers always abandon everyone who cares about them. Just like my parents deserted me."

April stared into eyes that had changed from rich chocolate to black ice. There didn't seem to be anything else to say. Tyler spoke from such a well of pain there was no room for an idea different from his own. She could talk until her hair turned gray, and he would never change his mind.

She had sensed his disapproval of her. At least now she knew why he felt that way. He might condescend to kiss her and even like it, but he would always think she was irresponsible and unreliable.

April sighed and walked over to the table. She turned the little box of matches end over end as she tried to collect her thoughts. Finally, she picked them up and stowed them in her arm pouch. Matches might be useful on the trip down the mountain. There was nothing she could do about the way Tyler felt about her. It was time to move on.

"I'll go get my stuff out of the other room. Is there anything else we should take with us?" she asked.

"Not that I can think of. I'll look around and see if I can find anything useful. We drove for a long time. It's going to be one hell of a walk."

April went into the smaller room and gathered her belongings. She put her helmet in her shoulder bag and holstered her radio. It had survived the assault on the window with only a few scratches. She couldn't feel any cracks or dents; maybe it would work when she got back to civilization.

Carrying the kerosene lamp, Tyler entered the room. He held the lantern high to illuminate the entire space, but there was nothing to be seen but dirt, cobwebs and their scuffed footprints in the dust on the floor. April thought sadly of the embrace they had shared there. *How could a kiss have felt so wonderful and meant so little?*

Tyler turned without a word, and April followed him into the larger room. He gestured at a plastic container on the table after putting the lamp down. "I scrounged up an empty milk jug and filled it with water. We might need that. But I couldn't find anything else. Too bad they didn't leave us a couple of steaks. I could sure use one about now."

Right on cue April felt her own stomach rumble hollowly. She put her shoulder bag on the scarred table, sat down in one of the rickety chairs and rummaged through her bag. "I have a PowerBar in here somewhere." She pulled it out with a flourish. "Ta da! Dinner for two."

Tyler groaned and joined her at the table. "Four bites of pure dining pleasure."

April unwrapped the bar, then carefully broke it into two pieces. She held the halves up to measure their relative lengths then pinched off a tiny bit to make them perfectly equal. "Complain, complain. Haven't you ever heard about beggars and their choices?"

She handed Tyler one of the two pieces of the PowerBar plus the extra pinch. He popped his portion into his mouth and ate it in one big bite then rubbed his stomach. "There's nothing quite like a satisfying meal."

"You're right." April nibbled at one end of her piece of the PowerBar. She closed her eyes. "Shrimp cocktail." She took another tiny bite and smacked her lips appreciatively. "Fettuccini Alfredo."

Tyler laughed. "I can hardly wait to see what happens when you get to dessert."

April grinned at him then licked the last few morsels from the wrapper. "Chocolate Decadence, of course," she said, squeezing her face into a caricature of perfect bliss.

The ecstatic look faded away as she thought about how far they were from home. Who knew how long it would be before they got back to the previously taken-for-granted comforts of fast food and supermarkets?

"Do you think anybody is looking for us yet?" she wondered aloud.

"Not unless someone thought the way Harmon and Willis took you away in the van looked suspicious enough to call the police. They suckered me in an alley. Not much chance of that being reported."

"What about your office staff? Or maybe... a wife?"

April held her breath waiting for his answer. Never once had she thought Tyler might be married. But of course he could be, probably was, in fact. She forced herself to breathe out slowly. What difference did it make? Her anxiety over his marital state was totally unwarranted.

"No wife. Not yet anyway," he said cockily.

April looked down at the table and frowned. *What did that mean? Is he engaged?* She viciously twisted the PowerBar wrapper into a tortured coil.

"I told my assistant I was leaving for the day," he continued. "It's Friday. She won't start checking on me until Monday, and I didn't have anything planned for the weekend where I'd be missed. What about you?"

He didn't care enough about whether she had a husband or not to ask specifically, she noted. He probably didn't think a "thrill seeker" like her could ever catch a husband anyway. She should tell him her five kids were probably crying their eyes out at this very moment.

"I live alone," she admitted. "No one will look for me yet."

"Not even the messenger service? Don't you have to check in at the end of the day?"

"We're supposed to. To turn in the package tags from our deliveries. Otherwise we don't get paid. But couriers are known for being... " She struggled for a word that wouldn't sound derogatory but couldn't come up with one that was exactly right. She tipped her head and shrugged ruefully. "... eccentric. The dispatcher probably didn't think too much about it, when I didn't go back to the office. I imagine she thought I'd decided to get a jump start on the weekend."

Tyler put his hands flat on the table, pushed his chair back and stood up. "So. It's up to us." He picked up the kerosene lamp. "It'll be damned awkward carrying this thing, but it's the only light we have." He looked inquiringly at April. "Do you have all your things? Are you ready to go?"

She nodded and with feigned heartiness replied, "Sure. Let's do it!"

She stood, put the water jug in her shoulder bag, slung the pack over her shoulders, walked to the door and stepped outside.

Moonlight silvered the towering firs and lacy ferns, creating a fantasy landscape. A slight breeze stirred boughs of massive spruce and pine, bringing the faint sound of dislodged raindrops and the pungent scent of juniper and cedar. Compared to the accustomed rush of city traffic and lights, the forest was eerily silent and dark.

April took her first step onto the trail that led down the mountain. It twisted and turned, appeared and disappeared among the trees, until far off in the distance it became a mere silver thread. It looked like it went on forever.

Five

Tyler stood in the doorway and watched April take her first few tentative steps along the path. Then she straightened her shoulders and picked up the pace, swinging along as though she didn't have a care in the world. He marveled at her courage. She could have been on a recreational day hike instead of fleeing from criminals who might come back at any moment to kill both of them.

She stopped to pick up a stick and poke it into a clump of salal at least a head taller than she was. She turned to him and called out, "Could you bring the lantern a little closer? Harmon threw my bike somewhere over here, but it's hard to see in the bushes."

Holding the lantern high, he joined her at the edge of the path. Turning in a slow half circle, he played the light as far as he could into the forest.

"There it is! My baby!" She hopped over low-growing Oregon-grape, ducked under a spruce and all but disappeared into a mammoth, dense growth of some kind of plant he didn't recognize. For her sake he hoped it wasn't poison oak.

"April, wait. I'll help."

But before he could even set the lantern down, she was carrying the bike through the forest, triumph written all over her face. "No need. I got it," she said proudly.

He couldn't help but smile at her pleasure over her feat. No wonder she didn't seem particularly concerned about whether the criminals would return. Tiny in stature but with the heart of a lion, April could probably take on a whole squadron of killers without batting an eyelash. He'd never known anyone like her. Even his fearless mother might have had a few qualms in a situation like this.

Tyler clenched his teeth at the fleeting thought of his mother. What kind of irrational impulse had possessed him when he spilled his guts to April about his parents? He never talked about them to anyone, ever. Only a wimp seeking sympathy—usually in an attempt to manipulate somebody else—went around telling sob stories about his rotten childhood.

Resolutely, he wrenched his thoughts back to the present. He could berate himself later for exposing his weakness. First, he needed to get her to safety, and maybe even more important, get himself safely away from her. Then he could figure out what it was about her that made him willing to share his painful past.

April put the bike down on the path, mounted it, slowly rode a few feet then stopped. She balanced in one place, shifting her weight from side to side, went forward more quickly, then repeated the whole procedure, checking the frame and tires, he supposed, finally circling back to where he stood holding the lantern.

"Is it okay?" he asked. He could see how important it was to her.

"Seems to be. I'll be able to tell better when I get on a straightaway."

She hopped off the bike with the grace of a deer. Her every move was a delight. How could he keep his mind on their escape when his body tightened just from watching her? But they had to get away from the cabin, the quicker the better. First, locate the blueprints, then get going.

He walked to where he thought the Lexus had been parked and tried to gauge exactly where he had crept into the forest. April followed. "I hope I can find the blueprints as easily as you did your bike," he said. "There wasn't much time to hide them."

"I don't see how you even got them out of the car, much less hid them, with your hands tied behind your back."

The admiration in her voice made him feel ridiculously pleased. A broken twig dangling from a bush caught his eye. He moved closer. Yes, he saw crushed ferns a little farther into the woods. "Here. It's this way, I think. I wrapped them in my raincoat and put them under a log."

April left her bike on the trail and slipped into the forest behind him. "Over there," she said, pointing at a monstrous downed fir covered with moss. "Is that it?"

He flashed the lantern in the direction she pointed. "No. It was older, more rotted."

He held the lamp higher to illuminate a wider arc. He groaned. At least half a dozen ancient crumbling logs littered the forest floor. And that was only what he could see from where they were standing just a few feet from the trail. He had no idea of how far he had fled into the forest before stashing the blueprints.

"Don't worry. We'll find them," April said, sounding considerably more confident than he was feeling at the moment. She zipped from one log to another with the speed of a hummingbird, moving unhesitatingly over and around the tumble of branches and debris. She quickly moved farther into the gloom than the lantern rays penetrated.

"Wait. Don't go so fast. You can't see; you'll hurt yourself." He crashed after her. Damn woman, always darting off without thinking or at least letting him know what she was going to do.

The woods seemed much denser than he remembered. He felt as clumsy as a bear as he struggled through the thickets. How had he hidden the blueprint tube with his hands tied behind him? But he knew. His fear that the thugs were going to hurt April had been a powerful motivation.

Suddenly, she materialized right in front of him, her face glowing with enough light to illuminate the whole forest. She thrust his raincoat and the case that held the blueprints toward him.

"I found them. Just a little piece of the sleeve was sticking out. You did a great job of hiding them."

Again, that thrill of pleasure at her compliment. He didn't want to care so much about what she thought of him. His reply sounded gruffer than he intended. "Don't you ever just walk where you're going? Next time how about waiting for me?"

The light in her face was extinguished as completely as if he had snuffed out a candlewick. "I'm sorry. I didn't mean... " she stammered. "I just thought the quicker we found the blueprints the quicker we could leave." She dropped her hands and sighed, then reached over her shoulder to stow the raincoat and blueprint tube in her pack.

Tyler sighed, too, exasperated with himself, and turned back toward the trail. He felt like a heel. She had accomplished their goal, and he had practically bitten her head off. And she was the one apologizing? Of course, she wanted to get away from here as fast as she could and probably away from him, too, as far and as fast as was humanly possible.

They reached the trail. Compared to the gloom of the forest interior, the path seemed almost well lit.

"I'm going to blow the lantern out," he said. "I think there's enough moonlight to see where we're going right now, and we might need the light more later."

"It is fairly bright out here," she agreed. "I think we can manage without the lamp."

April retrieved her bike and started down the mountain. Tyler paused long enough to turn the screw on the side of the lantern to lower the wick, lift the glass cover and blow out the flame. After he replaced the cover, he caught up with April.

Now he was sorry he'd doused the light. The lantern made her hair glow like a fiery sun, but the moon only picked out an occasionally glint from the mass of copper. He remembered how soft her curls had felt against his fingers. Almost as soft as her lips against his mouth.

Tyler swallowed hard. Dangerous thoughts. April was beautiful, but he couldn't let his attraction to her blind him to the kind of person she was: impulsive, chaotic and ultimately heart breaking.

Sure, she was a great ally in a tight spot, but a woman who faced danger with courage was the same woman who would face the routine so necessary to a good home life with restlessness. And how long would it be before that restlessness grew until it was more important than anything else, and she was off to somewhere new and exciting, leaving her devastated husband and children behind?

He wanted to get closer to April, but he knew better. He could admire her spirit and beauty, but he needed to maintain a safe distance. She was the wrong kind of woman for him.

If only he hadn't kissed her. It had been a monumental mistake. Now all he could think of was his desire to kiss her again. And again.

Tyler ducked to avoid a low branch and sighed once more. At that level he had a perfect view of April's delightful, curvaceous bottom frisking along the path only a few tantalizing feet ahead of him. He felt the involuntary tightening of his body and jerked his gaze away. He should have let the branch slap him in the face. Tiny April Thompkins presented more of a threat to him than all the murderers in the whole state of Washington.

April heard the sigh and wondered what Tyler was thinking about right now. If the sigh stemmed from frustration, she could certainly identify with that. She was experiencing major frustration herself.

She squeezed the handgrips on the Cannondale's handlebars as hard as she could. It was all she could do to prevent herself from leaping on the bike and dashing down the steep incline. After all, it was a mountain bike, perfect for this terrain. She could be back to civilization and help in no time at all.

But what about Tyler? One part of her longed to be flying away, the wind sharp in her face, on her own with the glorious sense of freedom she loved. But another equally strong part of her wanted to be right where she was with this exasperating man who told her not to go so fast—to slow down and wait for him.

She hadn't wanted to run away when he held her in his arms. All she could think of then was his warmth and strength and her own longing to get closer to him, brand new feelings for her; she didn't know how to deal with them. She'd never met a man before who could hold her interest for more than a few moments. Oh, sure, she'd feel a prickle of lust every once in a while, but usually the man who inspired speculation on how he'd perform out of his clothes turned out to be an idiot or just too much trouble to be worth the bother to find out.

On the surface Tyler seemed like a major pain in the butt, too, so why couldn't she just forget about him and zoom on down the mountain? For a moment she wanted to get away so badly she could actually see herself on the bike yards ahead of where she was now, jolting over holes and rocks, turning her head just enough to yell back that she'd send help. Which she would, of course.

She kicked a rock in the path and listened to it clatter down the slope. She felt torn.

While she was debating, a cloud moved over the moon, shuttering the light they'd used for traveling. At the same moment, an owl hooted in the distance. April shivered and stopped walking.

Ultimately, what she wanted to do didn't really matter anyway. She couldn't leave Tyler to make his way down the mountain alone. She would never leave anyone alone in this spooky place.

She turned to Tyler. "I can't see. Do you think we should light the lantern again?"

"We've been walking close to an hour. I don't think we should try to walk all night. We need some rest, and we'd make better time in the daylight anyway."

"But what if Harmon and Willis come back?"

Tyler cautiously made his way to the edge of the trail. He pushed a pine bough aside and tried to peer into the forest. "We're far enough away from the cabin, that if we get off the path, I don't think there'd be any chance of them finding us. The problem is to find a place to sleep without breaking our necks."

April took the matches out of her arm pouch and handed them to Tyler. "Here. We need to use the lantern to find a camping spot."

Tyler lit the lamp. "Look for a rocky place where there isn't much growing. I doubt if Willis and Harmon are all that great at tracking, but the less trail we leave behind us the better."

They walked a few more feet side by side in silence, then April pointed to two large trees spaced fairly far apart. "How about over there? See all the little pebbles."

"All right. Let's try it."

April followed Tyler into the forest, carrying her bike so it wouldn't leave a tire track in the soft, wet ground. As far as she could tell in the poor light, the rocks and pine needles around them seemed to hide their footprints fairly well, though she wasn't sure how much evidence of their passage would be exposed in the full light of day.

They zigged and zagged through the woods to avoid the worst of the underbrush, until April was totally confused. She would hate to wager much money on her chance of finding the road again if she were by herself.

She paused to put the bike down for a moment. Exhaustion was about to claim her. She knew her strength well, but she also knew her limit, and she had just about reached it. She pulled out her bandanna to wipe the sweat from her forehead before it ran into her eyes.

She looked up as the moon reappeared from behind the clouds. The lofty top of a magnificent pine bisected the moon's perfect circle. She drew in a lungful of the exquisite cold piney air and let it out.

The night was so frosty she could see her breath in the moonbeams, but fortunately, she was exercising hard enough to work up a sweat so she didn't feel cold at all.

April blinked. Moonbeams? She could see the little puffs of cloud formed by her breathing in the moonlight, but where was the lantern? Where was Tyler?

She spun around scanning her surroundings, but all she saw were trees and ferns. She held herself very still. The only sounds she heard were her ragged breathing, the soughing of branches and the faint babble of water running over stones.

"Tyler? Tyler, where are you?" she called.

Nothing. A knot of fear clenched her stomach. When had she last seen the lantern's flickering light? She had been looking at the ground, trying to avoid the gnarled roots rising to trip her and thorny brambles reaching out to shred her clothes and rip her skin.

Could Tyler have fallen over a cliff? Drowned in a river? Surely, Willis and Harmon hadn't found him. It wasn't possible.

But if something had happened to Tyler, she would have heard him call out, or at the very least heard a crash or splash. How could he have disappeared so quickly and silently? And why did she feel such total panic at the thought of him being gone?

Something rustled in the bushes behind her. April whirled around eagerly, her lips parted, ready with a relieved greeting. But Tyler wasn't there. Her spirits plummeted.

Staring hard at the spot where the sound had come from, she cautiously backed away. It must have been some stealthy night creature alarmed by her intrusion into his domain. A little frisson of fear shimmied up her spine, and the tiny hairs at the back of her neck stood on end. *Just what kind of animals live out here in the forest, anyway?* She knew there were deer and squirrels, but what about bears and cougars? Or maybe snakes?

Tremors started to shake her muscles in a classic fight-or-flight syndrome, but she willed herself to control her fear. She forced her gaze from where the sound had emanated. "Tyler," she called softly, not wanting to disturb any more wild things, "please answer me."

"Over here, April."

She felt almost dizzy with the relief that coursed through her body. The voice came from a distance, but it was unmistakably Tyler's. She walked toward the sound.

"All right. You're heading in the right direction. No, not over there. You're getting colder. This way, April."

Her sense of relief changed to irritation. *Where is he, anyway? Why doesn't he just show himself?*

"Okay, now you're getting warmer." His voice was more distinct. And the sound of running water was also much louder. "Closer, closer, you're getting hot. Hotter, hotter. Red hot!"

Totally exasperated, April stopped by a towering wall of rock, put her hands on her hips and pursed her lips. She had found the source of the water. It cascaded in a frothy torrent down the face of the cliff into a gorge at her right to form a wide stream. But still no sign of Tyler.

She was going to give him a good smack if she ever found him. She was furious over his playing this silly game when she had been so worried about him.

"Tyler Nielsen, if you don't come out right now, I'm going to leave you here all by yourself!"

The branches of a fir, that grew up against the rock wall, began to sway unnaturally. April stepped back. Tyler popped out from between the boughs, a smile as wide as the Columbia River stretched across his face.

"In here. I found a cave!" His voice was as excited as an eight-year-old's.

April's anger melted away. How could she be mad at him, when he sounded like a little boy on Christmas day? She might have to revise her opinion of Tyler as stuffy businessman. It seemed he was capable of letting his guard down, after all, and having a good time even in this most unlikely of situations.

Tyler held the branches to one side. "Come on in. It's dry, and there's enough room for your bike. We might even be able to start a little fire to warm up."

April ducked under the branches and tilted her bike at an angle to worm it in under the tree. Tyler had left the lantern burning in the cave, so once she was well under the fir, she could clearly see the yawning entrance, even though there had been absolutely no sign of either light or cave, when she had been standing at the outside edges of the thick branches of the tree.

She edged into the opening in the rock wall and wrestled the bike in after her. The roof of the cave was low; she couldn't stand up straight, and the entrance was small, but once inside, the cave opened up into a fairly roomy space. She couldn't see how far into the cliff the cave extended, but it was deep enough that the lantern light failed to penetrate into its dark recesses.

April pushed the bike toward the back of the cave, dropped her shoulder bag and sank gratefully to the rocky cavern floor. Exhaustion pulled at her, making her arms and legs heavy and limp. And now that she was no longer generating heat by hiking over rough ground, she could already feel the bone-numbing cold invading her body. She shivered.

Tyler's face instantly registered concern. "I'll get a fire started. The cliff comes down over the cave in a kind of shelf, so when I found the entrance, there were some twigs and dead leaves piled up that had drifted in and stayed dry under the overhang. I gathered them up, while you were looking for me."

Her teeth chattering, April gave Tyler the matches. He quickly built a pyramid of dried evergreen needles, leaves, twigs and broken branches. To her surprise, he seemed quite the woodsman. In no time a cozy blaze warmed and lit the cavern. The smoke lazily drifted toward the cave opening.

April scooted closer to the fire and stretched her fingers toward the welcome warmth. She loosened her shoes, took them off and thrust her cold feet and wet socks almost into the flames.

She wiggled her toes and let out a sigh of relief. Her feet had taken quite a beating today. It felt wonderful to finally be at rest.

She was massaging her feet, trying to rub the numbness away, when she heard the first pattering of rain outside. She and Tyler both looked toward the entrance. A curtain of rain poured from the overhanging ledge of rock, and a boom of thunder reverberated through the cliff walls.

April ducked when she heard the loud crack. "Am I ever glad we're not out there now!" A gust of cool, rain-scented air stirred the ashes at the edge of the fire. April realized the interior of the cave was already several degrees warmer than outside. The rocky walls reflected back the heat. "It's nice and cozy in here," she said contentedly.

Tyler nodded his agreement, looking proud. "I was lucky to find the cave."

"How did you find it, anyway? When I was looking for you, I was staring right at it and didn't see anything."

A dusky red crept up Tyler's neck. Funny, she'd never noticed before how attractive a blush could be on a man. "I needed a few minutes of privacy—a call of nature," he mumbled. "I didn't want you to walk up on me unexpectedly so I hid between the cliff and the tree and saw the cave."

She grinned at his discomfiture, but the grin turned into a yawn. She was so tired. Her eyelids sagged, seemingly of their own weight, and she leaned back on her arms into an arch to stretch the soreness out of her back. She could already feel her damp, sticky clothing begin to dry out.

She opened her eyes and caught Tyler staring at her. With a guilty look on his face, he hurriedly turned to the lantern to put it out and cleared his throat as though there were something stuck in it. "There's hardly any fuel left," he said in a husky voice. "It won't be worth the bother to take it with us tomorrow."

April pulled her feet back from the fire, wrapped her arms around her legs and rested her chin on top of her knees. "Do you think we'll be off the mountain by tomorrow night?"

Tyler removed his shoes and set them aside before answering. The once-fine leather was stained with mud and water. They were beautiful business shoes but hardly what anyone would pick for a trek through the mountains. Even so, she hadn't heard a word of complaint from him.

He settled cross-legged across the fire from her. The lightweight navy wool of his trousers, now damp and clinging from their hike, pulled tight across his muscular thighs, outlining them and other assets in the same general area. April jerked her gaze away.

Tyler scrubbed his hands roughly across his face. "I wish I knew. There were so many switchbacks on the way to the cabin it made it hard to judge the distance we traveled. It seems like a pretty isolated spot, but surely a few people live somewhere along the road."

"And if they don't?"

Tyler ran his hands through his hair to push it away from his face. April admired the way the firelight danced through the dark curls. She wished she were the one smoothing them off his forehead. He sighed. "Then I suppose we'll have to walk all the way to the shore. There have to be people down there."

April moved away from the fire and scrambled on hands and knees over to her shoulder bag. She pulled out the plastic jug of water, carried it back to the fire and offered it to Tyler.

He took it gratefully. "Thanks. I'm parched."

He tipped his head back and gulped down a healthy slug of water. Watching the muscles in his throat contract and the firelight warm his smooth olive skin and play over the rugged planes of his cheek and jaw, April felt her own throat constrict painfully.

Tyler lowered the jug and wiped his mouth with the back of his hand. April saw that his fingers were long and blunt and his wrist thick and powerful with dark hair beginning at the prominent knob of wrist bone and disappearing into his once-white shirt cuff. They were French cuffs with simple gold and onyx cufflinks.

As she greedily took in every detail of his appearance, she felt an unfamiliar tightening in her lower body. It was as though she hungered for any crumb of information about him, no matter how minute. She rubbed her arms and legs before the fire, pretending to warm them, to hide her quaking. She'd never before reacted to a man like this. It was scary.

Tyler passed the water jug to April. He thought he'd never seen anything so beautiful as this lithe young woman basking in the glow of the campfire.

As she stretched and warmed herself, she reminded him of a ginger kitten he'd once coveted when he was a boy. A school friend's mother cat had had a huge litter, but only one of the tiny kittens had been that particular shade of gingery reddish yellow. He'd begged his grandmother to let him have it, but she'd turned him down cold. To save his feelings, she'd said. It would only hurt him in the long run when it ran away or got hit by a car.

He shifted restlessly. April's eyes seemed to follow his movements. Could she be as aware of him as he was of her? Tension crackled through the cave, tension that didn't have anything to do with being stranded far from home.

He moved again, unable to sit still. His grandmother had probably been right, but it hadn't cured the wanting. The same way he wanted

April right now. His whole body ached with longing. He wanted to touch and kiss and stroke her until he kindled a roaring fire a thousand times hotter than the flames here in their little shelter.

April took a last sip of water, capped the plastic jug and set it aside. A drop of moisture clung to her lip and sparkled in the firelight like a rare diamond. Thumbprints of fatigue smudged the creamy pale skin beneath her lower lashes, but the glorious green of her eyes was as fresh as any of the ferns outside.

He couldn't stop himself. He had to touch her. He moved around the fire and gathered her into his arms. She trembled, but she didn't pull away. He buried his hands in the riotous mass of copper curls. They were even softer than he remembered. Tenderly, he smoothed them away from her face. She stared into his eyes, her own open wide. She looked apprehensive, but surely he saw the beginning of trust there, too.

"April, April," he murmured.

He kissed her forehead, then her temples and her eyelids. Her long eyelashes fluttered shut in sweet surrender, and she moaned softly. His blood was boiling through his veins. He wanted to rip her clothes away, but he forced himself to go slowly, savoring every moment.

He smoothed his lips over the tiny freckles that dusted her nose and her high cheekbones, then worked his way down her velvety soft cheeks and throat. She tasted salty and sweet at the same time.

Finally, he found her mouth. She parted her lips for him, and their tongues touched. He plunged deeply inside. She responded in kind. Her mouth was wet and hot and eager. She moaned deep in her throat, and he heard a roaring in his ears.

He unzipped her jacket. She wore a wildly patterned cartoon jersey underneath it. He nuzzled her breasts through the cotton. They were impossibly soft. He had to feel her skin. He pushed her shirt up. His breath caught in his throat when he discovered she wore no bra. Her breasts were small but perfectly formed and achingly beautiful, and her skin was as smooth and lovely as the finest satin.

He wanted to rip and rage and tear like some wild beast that might have actually mated at one time in this cave, but with the greatest of effort he willed restraint. April was trembling like a slim, pale aspen in a gale. He guessed she had little experience with men—she seemed so innocent and hesitant. But he couldn't stop the growl that tore through his throat as he lowered his mouth to the dusky pink buds that beckoned with a siren call.

April gasped when his lips touched her breast. She arched her back, and her head fell back as though she could no longer support its weight. She writhed in his arms, thrusting her breasts against his face. She was so small, so perfect, so utterly delectable. He felt as though he could gobble her up in one bite.

Tyler pulled back. He tried to engage his brain. He'd been acting on pure lust, nothing but animal instinct. He was panting, and he was so aroused he felt as though he might explode at any moment, but he couldn't go on with this.

Why not? he thought desperately. Why couldn't he, for once, just give into what he wanted so badly?

He shook his head to clear the fog of desire and tried to think. He was pulled to April by an attraction stronger than any he had ever felt for any other woman, but she wasn't right for him. She wasn't the woman he had been seeking for so long. They would be home soon, hopefully the next day, and they would never see one another again.

At the very thought, Tyler felt something latch on to his heart and squeeze until he could barely breathe, but he ignored the pain. April would be off to some brand-new, hare-brained job, risking life and limb, and he would go back to his business and his plans.

Back to Nancy Simmons.

He groaned, no longer with desire but in despair. Why did that sound like some kind of jail sentence? She had been what he wanted this morning. Why couldn't he have what he wanted right now, too?

A one-night stand. Why not? He'd had them before in his life. They were two consenting adults. *A little pleasure after a very trying day. What would be so wrong about a one-night stand?*

At his groan April's eyes had shot open. "What's the matter? Did I do something wrong?"

Her impossibly long, pale eyelashes trembled shyly, but her stunning grass-green eyes registered nothing but trust. She trusted him. He couldn't possibly take advantage of such innocence.

He wanted to take her here on the rocky cave floor more than anything he'd ever wanted before, but he couldn't do it. It wouldn't be right to use her merely to satisfy his lust, to rid himself of the fire she'd ignited in his blood, then abandon her. He couldn't hurt her that way.

He took a deep breath. Carefully, gently, he smoothed her jersey back in place and zipped her jacket back up. It was one of the hardest things he'd ever done.

"No, April, you didn't do anything wrong. But we need to rest. We have a hard day ahead of us tomorrow. This isn't the right time for... for what we were doing," he finished lamely.

He saw the hurt on her face. He half expected her to lash out at him, but she didn't. She pulled herself up proudly and regally withdrew the few feet to the other side of the fire. It might have been a continent away. He felt hollow. His whole body ached.

He moved toward April's shoulder bag. "Do you mind if I get my raincoat? I thought we could use it as a kind of sleeping bag."

She still didn't deign to answer him, and he didn't blame her. She just nodded her assent. He felt like a jerk. But not as much of a jerk as if he had made love to her, knowing all the time they could have no future.

He busied himself with spreading his raincoat by the fire. There were only a few branches left. He gestured toward the dwindling pile of kindling. "Let's save what wood we have for tomorrow. We can build a little fire to warm up before we get started."

Still no answer. Damn. He shook his head regretfully. There was no way around it. "So, I guess we should roll up in the raincoat together." No response. "To conserve body heat. The fire will burn out soon."

As majestically as a queen settling into the royal four-poster, April lay down on the raincoat. Tyler joined her. She nestled spoon-style against his back, curving her body around him into a perfect fit. Tyler pulled the raincoat up over them and gritted his teeth.

She squirmed into a more comfortable spot. Her breasts caressed his back. Visions of their recently uncovered beauty danced through his head, far more enticing than any sugarplum fairies, and his trousers seemed to shrink three sizes into a painfully tight fit. She was probably just moving to avoid a pebble, but if she was trying to torture him for revenge, she was doing an excellent job of it.

What a terrible idea sleeping together in his raincoat had been. Better to have frozen to death. There would be no rest for him tonight.

Six

April picked her way over the rocky slope leading down to the mountain stream. A wash of faint pink bled across the pale blue sky. Tendrils of fog still curled around the shaggy evergreens but promised to burn off soon. Yesterday's dark clouds had been cleared away by the night's rain.

April yawned and reached for the sky in a long, languorous stretch. It was going to be a glorious day. Too bad she was too muddled to enjoy it.

As she stood at the edge of the creek, watching the gurgling water wearing away at the boulders, she pondered her confused feelings for Tyler. Last night he had seriously wounded her when he had so abruptly turned away from their lovemaking. What was it about her that bothered him? Was she so repellent that he'd been unable to continue after the initial impulsive kiss?

They were consenting adults with, as far as she could tell, no previous commitments. Why had he pulled away from her?

Shaking her head in frustration, she fumbled in her pocket for her bandanna, squatted by the stream and gritted her teeth as she prepared for the icy shock of the water.

She dipped the cloth in the creek, rung it out, rubbed it across her face, then wiped the sleep from her eyes. Shivering in anticipation, she rinsed the bandanna, wrung it out again and reached up under her jacket and jersey to wash her body. She gasped at the touch of the frigid cloth, but it felt good to be almost clean again.

She hopped up and down and beat her arms against her sides to warm up, then started back up the creek bank toward the cave, her mind racing with memories of the previous evening.

She knew she didn't have much sexual expertise with men. It had been a long time since she'd been with anyone, and her few encounters had mostly been fumbling teenage experiments, anyway. Perhaps it was her inexperience and ineptitude that had turned Tyler off.

She'd always planned to have a serious relationship someday, but it seemed she never got around to it. There were always too many other interesting things to do, and she knew a commitment tied you down. A relationship took time, lots and lots of time.

Look at her mother, for example, and her sisters and aunts. Their husbands and families seemed to suck their very life away. If any of them had even a half an hour a day they could call their own, it was a small miracle.

Not that any of them were complaining. Now that April thought about it, she realized they were actually a disgustingly contented lot. It was hard to imagine, but if you believed the glow of happiness on their faces, true. There had to be something in the picture she was missing.

April sighed. A slender downed tree lay in her path. She hopped up on it, spread her arms for balance and walked tightrope fashion along the trunk.

Even though she'd never had a serious romance, she'd still always had lots of boys, and then men, for friends. She always figured she could have a lover if she really wanted one. The trouble was, she had never found a man she wanted enough to waste that much time on him.

A series of huge rocks blocked her way up the bank. Just for the fun of it, she clamored up the first boulder and leaped from one to another. It almost felt like flying. It cheered her up a little but not much.

She pivoted on top of the biggest rock and surveyed her wild surroundings. Dozens of shades of green from ferns, trees and moss normally would have delighted her, but even though her eyes registered the feast of primitive beauty, her emotions remained detached. Now all she could think of was Tyler.

Okay, so he thought she led a frivolous lifestyle, that she wasn't a good marriage candidate. Though why he had to point that out to her right when they'd been going at it hot and heavy she couldn't fathom. She hadn't thought there were that many people still around who thought you had to make a marriage proposal before you could touch. He was either unbelievably principled or a sanctimonious prig.

So, why didn't he like her enough to make love to her? She wasn't really all that repulsive—was she?

She stopped twirling on the boulder long enough to look down at her body and catalog her assets. She fluffed up her sleep-matted hair and twisted at the waist to see her backside.

Well, she was awfully skinny and had no breasts to speak of and maybe her bottom was proportionally too big compared to the rest of her, but still... there had been too many boys and, when she grew older, men who had acted as though they were interested in her for her to have ever worried about it.

She distorted her face in a moue of distaste just thinking about how silly some of them had behaved. It had never taken her more than two minutes to set any of them straight, though, she thought with satisfaction, and she'd managed to keep most of them for friends, too.

When she was little, April and her would-be boyfriends had all gone back to building forts after she'd rejected them, and when she was grown up, she and her wanna-be lovers were usually involved in a work project or sporting event, so the men could save face by pretending they'd never made a pass at all.

But with Tyler it was different.

She jumped down from the boulder and started back up the hill. Her heart beat in a strange cadence just thinking about him, and it had nothing to do with the exertion of climbing the creek bank.

Everything was topsy-turvy with Tyler. Unlike her past suitors, he had rejected her.

As she remembered how he had pulled away from her, she had to stop walking and squeeze her eyes shut against the wave of dizziness and pain that threatened to overwhelm her. The emotion was so strong, she felt as though she were falling down into a deep, dark well. But she had a safety rope to hang onto.

She took a long, shuddering deep breath. Her safety rope was the knowledge that, in spite of last night's rejection, she was pretty sure Tyler wanted her as much as she wanted him no matter what he said or did. The tremor in his voice and hands and the passion lighting his dark eyes had given him away. That had to mean desire—didn't it?

Which brought her right back around to the beginning of the puzzling circle of her thinking. So, why, then, had he rejected her? She sighed. It was just too confusing.

"Good morning, April."

She started. Looking up, she saw Tyler standing at the crest of the bank.

Be still, she admonished her heart, which was threatening to pound right out of her chest at the sight of him. She waved a greeting and slowed her pace, none too anxious to see how he would behave after their evening encounter.

Tyler didn't approve of her, she knew. Somehow, she reminded him of a terrible grief from his past. He thought she was wild, foolish, maybe even a little crazy.

But he definitely wanted her. She was convinced of that. And for the first time in her life, she wanted back.

Pausing to catch her breath, she shaded her eyes against the brightening sky and watched Tyler take off his jacket and shirt to splash water from the cascading falls on his face and arms. Her throat constricted. She tried to swallow.

Dark hair coursed across his chest and down his belly. He was rock hard with well-defined biceps and pectorals and a washboard stomach. He was utterly gorgeous.

With great effort she managed to tear her gaze away to watch where she was walking so she wouldn't catapult back down the steep bank.

Too bad they were all wrong for one another.

For once in her life she hadn't chosen to go on this particular adventure. Fate, taking the form of a set of blueprints, had snatched her up and deposited her in a wilderness with a luscious hunk of a man. But now that she was here, she was tempted to take advantage of the situation. It would be a perfectly good time for a fling. She could finally discover why people made such a fuss over sex. Surely, if she put her mind to it, she could overcome his scruples or pain or whatever was holding him back and seduce him.

She risked a peek at Tyler. Drat! He'd put his shirt and jacket back on. She looked down at the ground and shook her head, scolding herself for her foolishness.

True, she liked risk, but only after she had calculated the odds and was convinced that with skill, determination and guts she would win. She wasn't absolutely certain she could win at this game.

Tyler was too dangerous. He set her blood aflame with a single touch. She reacted to him too strongly, and the only outcome she could see was pain.

Even if she was able to tempt him into making love to her, nothing good could ever come of it. They were just too different. No, she didn't want to make love to Tyler, no matter how much he excited her, knowing all along it would be a one-night stand. If she made love, she wanted it to be with someone she could respect the next day. She almost laughed. *Isn't that supposed to be the woman's line?*

She raised her head, straightened her shoulders determinedly and walked more briskly up the slope. She had to stick with Tyler until they got home, and that would be the end of it. Then he could go back to his boring business, and she could forget all about him. They would never meet again.

That made her stop. She put her hand on her chest. Breathing pained her. Strange how much it hurt, the thought of never seeing Tyler again.

Maybe it's time to try a new occupation. A challenge would help her forget Tyler's kisses, and even if a new job wasn't quite up to that task, well, she was getting a little old to be a bike courier, anyway.

Ruefully, she massaged her neck. Yesterday's strenuous demands had taken more of a toll on her body than she cared to admit. A variety of aches and pains clamored for her attention, but she ignored them. She had more important thoughts on her mind.

Slowly, she crested the rise. Tyler had finished his grooming. His dark hair was slicked back and glistening with water, and his olive skin was ruddy from the cold. In spite of the cuts and bruises on his face, he looked strong, healthy and very, very male.

He stood waiting for her with barely restrained impatience, his fists clenched rigidly at his sides. He scowled at her.

"Where were you?" he asked, sounding decidedly grouchy.

"You know where I was. You called down to me," she answered with patient logic.

"But I didn't know when I got up in an empty cave while it was still barely dawn, did I? I wouldn't think I'd have to point this out to you, April, but like it or not, we're stranded in a wilderness together. Wilderness, as in wild. So it's only the most basic of survival rules for us to practice some kind of buddy system. That means you don't go traipsing off somewhere without telling me where you're going. Agreed?"

She rolled her eyes skyward in a quick plea for forbearance. "Boy, did somebody get up on the wrong side of the campfire, or what?"

He narrowed his eyes and pressed his lips together in a skinny unbecoming line, as though he were trying to prevent himself from shouting before he repeated stiffly, "Agreed?"

April raised her shoulders in a tiny, resigned shrug. "Okay."

Once he had wormed an agreement out of her, the tension in his body seemed to dissipate a little. A grin tugged at the corners of his mouth, threatening to erode his stern expression. "So, did the deer and rabbits enjoy your morning performance? Just what ballet was that, anyway? Swan Lake?"

She could feel a pink deeper than the glow from her icy bath suffuse her face. "You were spying on me!"

"I was not spying. I was looking for you. I thought you might be lying at the bottom of a gully somewhere with a broken leg, or worse."

He paused. His tone of indignation softened to a husky warmth that, in spite of all her efforts to ignore it, triggered a tightening in April's lower body. "You make a lovely dancer," he murmured.

She reddened. She tried to turn his compliment into a joke, but her voice betrayed her. "You make a pretty good-looking failed boxer yourself."

She moved closer to him and traced the outer edge of a cut on his chin with her little finger. The wounds were already beginning to close. He looked much better today, but standing so near him had been an error.

Tyler's hand captured her upraised wrist, and he pulled her up against him. His much greater size enfolded and warmed her. He felt hard, solid and wonderful. In an instant her breathing accelerated, and her resolve to avoid a romantic entanglement crumbled. *Would it really hurt anything to enjoy his kisses?*

She came to her senses not a moment too soon, as Tyler lowered his head until his mouth was only a fraction of an inch from hers. His ragged breathing warmed her lips. She jerked away.

She said the first thing that came into her head to break the tension. Her voice came out in a tight squeak. "We need to eat. Let's see if we can find some food."

He stared at her for what seemed like an eternity, his eyes dark and intense.

It was clear his hunger was for something other than food. For a moment April felt a thrill of triumph. She was right! He did want her in the same way she wanted him!

But her sense of victory vanished as quickly as it had come. The tension that pulled at them would make it just that much harder to get home safely with her self-esteem and her heart intact.

Finally, he looked away. Perhaps in an effort to pull himself together, he stooped, picked up a stone and hurled it with admirable pitching ability at a huge old madrona. There was a thunk and a sharp crack, then a branch dropped to the ground.

"If there are any rabbits around, I could pick one off for breakfast," he said.

April grimaced. "Not a bunny! I'd rather starve."

He smiled at her with a little boy's lopsided grin that made her bones melt. He patted his stomach ruefully. "From the sounds coming from my gut, I'd say that's an option that'll be here soon."

April went to the cave and gathered her belongings. Then they made their way through the forest toward the road.

"Look, over there," April said, pointing at a pool formed by backwater from the creek. "Cattails. You can eat them... I think."

"You think? That doesn't sound very reassuring. You're not trying to poison me, are you?"

She was grateful for the lighter tone. She answered in kind with mock indignation. "Of course not. I'll even take the first bite."

She scrambled down the embankment and began pulling up the tall, green, strap-like blades, trying, unsuccessfully, to keep her feet dry at the boggy water's edge. She washed the roots off and nibbled gingerly at the pale lower stem of one of the newer shoots.

"Well," she said doubtfully, "it doesn't taste too bad, I guess. Sort of like cucumber."

He smacked his lips in mock appreciation. "Great. Sort-of cucumber for breakfast. Sounds like a real treat."

She bit into another root. "Shut up, Nielsen, and eat. You'll need the strength to keep up with me today."

He laughed with infectious good humor. April felt her spirits rise. When he chose to joke with her, Tyler could make their ordeal almost seem like a holiday camping trip.

"Look over there, Tyler." She pointed at a small, tree-like shrub nestled next to a clump of salmonberry bushes that were already in bloom with lovely blossoms that looked like wild rose.

"There are still a few berries left that made it through the winter. I think it's some kind of cranberry. Why don't you make yourself useful and pick some for us?" she suggested. "You know, your contribution to breakfast, since there don't seem to be any ferocious bunnies lurking about for you to play warrior with. Those berries are edible, too. I think."

"Another 'I think'," Tyler grumbled, but he headed for the cranberry shrubs. "Sounds like a sure recipe for death to me."

April ignored his complaints and searched among the stones until she found one with a relatively sharp edge and used it to hack away at the stem and root ends of the cattails. When she'd gathered and washed a large bunch, she carried them to a moss-covered log surrounded by tiny new ferns, settled herself comfortably on it and waited for Tyler.

He joined her in the little glade, carrying his raincoat by the collar points and the lower corners, gathering it into a makeshift bag to hold the red and orange berries he had picked. Carefully, he unfolded the raincoat and spread it between them on the log to serve as a picnic tablecloth.

April added the cattails. Tyler sampled both.

"Not bad," he said, munching vigorously on a cattail root. "Starchy. Reminds me of the library paste I ate in school when I was a kid." He ate some more. "That certainly says something about how hungry I am."

April pursed her lips as she tasted the bitter fruit. "Wow! These berries sure put a pucker on."

With a twinkle in his eyes, Tyler lowered his head toward her lips. "Maybe they're kissing berries."

April jerked her head away.

Tyler grinned wickedly. "How did you learn so much about foraging?"

"Camp Waskowitz. Sixth grade," April said around a mouthful of milky white cattail root. "All blue berries are edible, some red berries are okay, and you never touch a white berry."

Tyler explosively spit a mouthful of red mush into the ferns. "These berries are red—the maybe group. And bitter as sin. How do you know they're okay?"

April smirked. She'd get even with him for trying to sneak a kiss when she wasn't prepared. "I don't. It's a maybe. I think it's some kind of cranberry, but maybe not. And sixth grade was a long time ago. I might have confused the colors a little."

He wiped the back of his hand across his mouth. "Amazing how I feel so full all of a sudden."

He leaned back against the thicker part of the log, swung his feet up and clasped his hands behind his head. He looked as relaxed and comfortable as a man in a hammock in his backyard.

He gazed at the sky. "Look, an eagle," he said, pointing.

She craned her head back just in time to see the regal bird swoop across a patch of blue between the evergreens. Its mighty wingspan seemed to fill the sky.

Her breath caught. It was magnificent.

When the eagle disappeared, she looked back at Tyler. He was watching her reaction to the bird. He nodded.

"This is the sort of thing I want to give to families at the mountain retreat I'm building."

"What do you mean?"

"The resort. The one the blueprints are for. The architectural plans that got us in this mess," he said wryly. "I want to make a place for families to go where they can get away from the city. A beautiful place where they can relax and unwind—learn a little bit about nature and a whole lot about each other. Help them become a stronger family."

"I like that," April said reflectively. "It's a nice idea. I guess I never thought of a resort in those terms before."

Tyler nodded. "It's the idea behind all my projects. Strengthening the family. The schools I design are meant to be welcoming, a place for the whole community to gather and support and be a part of."

Excited by the concept, breakfast forgotten, April hopped off the log. "That's super! Why, you're practically a philanthropist."

Tyler chuckled. "Hardly. I make money on my developments, you know. I don't give them away."

"Still. A humanitarian then. It doesn't sound like making money is the thing you're most interested in."

He grinned. "I have no complaints about making money. I don't mind having a little."

Then he spoke more seriously. "But you're right. The building is what really matters to me. It always has been."

A shadow crossed his face. "When I had to go live with my grandmother, she gave me a huge set of those little interconnecting log pieces you put together."

He ripped a piece of bark from the log and crumbled it between his fingers. "I used to build elaborate houses and pretend I lived in them with my parents—alive and well and actually wanting to stay home, of course. Then I had to build an appropriate town for our home. I covered my bedroom floor with make-believe buildings."

"Then when you grew up, you made them real," April said softly, pity for the lonely little boy tugging at her.

He stared into her eyes for a long moment then threw the bits of bark to the ground and rose from the log. "Did you know every single thing you think is reflected on your face, April? Just a moment ago you were as radiant as the sun, and now you look like you're going to weep for me."

She didn't know how to respond, but it didn't matter, because he didn't give her a chance. Carefully, as though she were made of the finest porcelain, he gathered her into his arms.

She knew she should pull away. Hadn't she just spent the entire morning deciding it was in everybody's best interest to avoid intimacy?

But as Tyler rained soft, gentle kisses on her face and neck, her resolve melted along with her knees. She was no longer capable of any kind of rational thought. All she could do was feel, and what Tyler was doing felt wonderful.

He ran his powerful hands all down her back and bottom and thighs. She arched into his caresses. The warmth and strength of his touch seemed to mold her. Her body became liquid and flowing. She wasn't sure her bones could support her much longer.

Tyler seemed to understand because he gently lowered her to the ground, to a bed of soft, tickly ferns and mosses that felt like a welcoming embrace.

He unzipped her jacket and pulled it, her arm pouch and her jersey off to trace slow kisses around the base of her breast. The kisses spiraled up and up until she thought she'd scream with anticipation. When he finally drew her nipple into his mouth, she moaned.

Tyler moaned, too, a guttural, primal cry. He pulled away from her long enough to tear off the suit coat that looked so out of place in the wilderness. He jerked his shirt buttons open and ripped off the stained and torn once-white shirt.

Her body shook in a frenzy of excitement. Her thoughts were disjointed and vague, but intuitively she sensed an underlying change in Tyler. As he shed his business costume, he seemed to strip away layers of inhibiting civilization until he reached a core of untamed, primitive man. He became a part of their environment, a wild savage creature capable of claiming the woman he wanted without a moment of hesitation.

She cried out his name in a thrill of fear and longing. He swooped back down to her like a fierce bird of prey.

The dark hair and broad chest that had seemed so tantalizingly far away only a few hours ago were suddenly within reach. With trembling fingers, she stroked his corded neck and explored a wandering path along his chest and abdomen all the way to his belt buckle.

He groaned and crushed her against him. He was hot and hard and overpoweringly male.

The rough texture of the hair on his chest rubbed against her already sensitized breasts. He plunged his tongue into her mouth, searching out secrets, seeking her essence. Her tongue answered him stroke for stroke. She had nothing to hide. She wanted to give him all of her, everything.

She perceived a stirring deep in her body, at the very core of her existence. She felt wild and free. A longing greater than anything she'd ever known overwhelmed her. She was burning with need. She wanted him. She needed him now.

A raucous chattering startled her. A squirrel clinging to a fir branch not far above their heads was scolding them with all the ferocity of a revivalist minister warning of the dangers of hell.

She tried to pull away. For a moment she tried to think reasonably, tried to remember all her arguments against getting close to this man. But it was too late. Only Tyler could put out the fire he had ignited.

When she hesitated, he paused, too. He stopped kissing her and moved just far enough away to look into her eyes. He seemed to be seeking an affirmation. No matter how wild and urgent their feelings, she was sure he would stop if she asked him to do so. But she didn't want him to stop.

She laced her fingers behind his neck and pulled his head back to her until their lips met again. His mouth was hot and demanding. "April," he murmured against her lips. "You make me crazy."

Without a fumble or missing an instant of their kisses, he unbuckled the belt of her radio holster and her fanny pack. He eased her bicycle tights and panties down and removed her shoes and socks.

Somehow, he had managed to make her clothes melt away. She was lying in the middle of a forest without a stitch on, and it felt absolutely right and wonderful. Except she needed Tyler to be even closer to her. She reached out to him to pull him to her.

His large powerful hands seemed to be everywhere at once, warming and kneading her body. He lavished attention on her thighs, her back, her arms, the arches of her feet. He worked his way down her body with hot, urgent kisses along her throat, her breasts, her belly.

The forest echoed with her cries. She couldn't stand it any longer. She had to have him inside her, her need was too great to bear. Wordlessly, incapable of talk, she clutched and scrabbled at his back and buttocks, trying to show him what she wanted.

He understood her inarticulate language. He must have felt the same way. He threw off his remaining clothing. April gasped at the sight of his powerful erection.

His eyes seemed to be burning. Her skin felt hot as his gaze ravaged her body.

And then he was exactly where she so desperately needed him to be. Without thinking, she opened her legs and her body for him. She was ready. He plunged home with one deep thrust.

For a single moment the forest seemed to hold its breath all around them. Then he began to move. April moaned and cried and begged. She seemed to be rushing through a void where nothing existed but Tyler and her. The passion grew and grew until it reached a wild crescendo.

Tyler's roar and her cry melded into a clamor that could have reached the heavens. The world seemed to explode—then it rained back down on them, as they lay twined together, satiated and replete.

But somehow a new feeling intruded. She could feel the exact moment it happened. The perfect mood was broken. Tyler moved away from her. Something was bothering him. His face twisted with his thoughts.

He got up, searched for her clothes, brought them over to her and laid them down at her feet. He spoke haltingly. She could see he was trying to be completely candid.

"I said you make me crazy, and you do. You're so full of fire and spirit and so very, very beautiful. I want you more than any woman I've ever known, but I can't offer you a future. I need a home... family... stability. And you can't be a part of that. You're too..."

He seemed to search for words. "I don't know... restless, I suppose. Impulsive and wild. I could never feel safe with you."

He pounded a clenched fist into his palm as though to punish his own flesh. "What I did was wrong. I knew it, but I did it anyway because I wanted you so much. I'm sorry. You aren't what I'm looking for," he concluded with brutal honesty.

April squeezed her eyes shut, trying to hold back the tears. She felt sick and disoriented. She covered her face with her hands. She didn't want him to know the power of his words, how much his rejection hurt.

She pressed her lips together to keep them from trembling. Struggling for dignity, she rubbed her hands across her face and ran them through her hair. She fought against the tremor that threatened to invade her voice. "I didn't ask for anything."

He swore under his breath, but whether it was at himself, the situation or her, she couldn't tell. "I know you didn't, April," he said aloud.

He rose to his feet in one fluid movement. She felt dwarfed and vulnerable, as he towered over her, but she couldn't seem to summon enough strength to get up.

He offered her his hand. She hesitated then took it. He pulled her up against his naked, warm body then quickly released her. The brief embrace left her aching and her senses reeling.

She was grateful when Tyler turned his back to her to put on his clothes, giving her a few moments to regain her composure. She dressed as quickly as she could, feeling exposed and vulnerable. The irony twisted her inside. Only a brief while ago her nudity had seemed perfectly natural.

Silently, April put the remaining cattails and berries in her shoulder bag, while Tyler refilled the plastic milk jug with water from the stream.

The sun shone brilliantly, hot enough to warm the chilly March air. A strong fragrance of pine and refreshed earth wafted up from the forest floor. Crystalline drops of water clung to the evergreen branches, reflecting flashes of sunlight. But for April, as she pushed and sometimes carried her bike through the underbrush, a gray pall hung over everything. She couldn't imagine ever laughing again.

It seemed to take an eternity to get back to the main road. Tyler was the first one to push through the branches to the dirt track. When April joined him, she saw an intent, worried expression on his face. A creepy-crawly sensation slithered up her spine.

"What is it?" she asked anxiously.

"Listen."

She strained her ears but heard nothing unusual, only the wind stirring through the trees.

"I don't hear any..."

Then she caught it. A still far away, but rapidly approaching, roar of motors.

Seven

"It might be help," Tyler said doubtfully.

April dropped her shoulder bag to the ground and leaped astride her bike. "Yes! It has to be. I'll go meet them."

Excitement trilled in her voice. Tyler felt something clench down tight around his heart when he realized how anxious she was to get away from him.

What was wrong with him? He should be just as relieved as she obviously was that this horror was almost over. Somehow the idea of getting back to his home and office wasn't as enticing as he had expected.

He put a cautionary hand on her shoulder. "Stay out of sight until we see who it is. It could be Willis and Harmon."

But she was too impatient to pay any attention to him. She shook his hand away. "It can't be. Remember what they said in the cabin? They're on their way to Tucson. There's no reason for them to come back here."

Before he could stop her, she flew off down the rough track of road. He ran a few steps after her. "April, wait!" But it was too late. The bike went too fast for him to catch her.

His foot caught in a branch covered over with dead leaves and pine needles, almost tripping him. He kicked the branch loose from its camouflage, picked it up and broke it over his knee in angry frustration. "Damn it all to..."

The curse died in his throat as an all-too-familiar black van nosed around the corner of a switchback.

"April, stop! It's their van," he screamed and tore after her.

The van was still fairly far down the mountain. There was a chance they wouldn't see April, if he could stop her in time.

Thank God! She must have heard him or seen the van herself because she jumped off the bike, thrust it into the underbrush beside the road and dove for cover after it.

Suddenly, Tyler remembered the shoulder bag lying alongside the trail. He reversed direction and raced back up the steep incline. His lungs burning, he grabbed the pack, pushed through heavy boughs of spruce and concealed himself behind a giant tree.

He watched as the van repeatedly vanished and reappeared along the switchbacks as it labored up the mountain. A dark sedan and his Lexus followed it.

He cursed softly. He hated seeing his own car being used by a gang of thugs. But then, it was still all in one piece. He'd supposed if he should ever see it again, it would be stripped as clean as a carcass attacked by a school of piranhas.

It was quite an entourage. Something was up that involved more than just Willis and Harmon.

A twig snapped behind him. He whirled, fists ready.

"Gotcha," April said, pointing an imaginary forefinger pistol at him. She had managed to sneak up only inches away, before he heard her.

His nostrils flared. "April! What a crazy thing to do. I might have hit you! In fact, I ought to smack..." He paused when he noted the tremor shaking her hand and the fear in her eyes.

Wordlessly, he opened his arms, and she threw herself into his embrace. He smoothed his fingers through her tangled curls, as she buried her face against his chest and squeezed him hard around his middle.

It was incredible. Even now, he felt himself respond, as her body pressed against him. She felt so right in his arms. He took a deep breath and let it out slowly. He wished he never had to move; he wished he could hold her like this forever.

She stirred in his arms and pulled in a shaky breath. He released her reluctantly. She tilted her head back to look up at him. Her beautiful green eyes were wide with apprehension. "Well, I guess we're still in for it, huh?" she said with a shiver.

He used his little finger to trace the spate of freckles that now appeared far more prominent than usual against her deathly pale skin. "Seems that way," he couldn't help but agree. But he'd make sure she was safe, if it was the last thing he did.

He pulled her beside him to crouch at the base of a hemlock with low-growing branches that nearly skimmed the ground. "I don't think they'll see us, if we stay down here and don't move."

April clutched his hand, as they watched the agonizingly slow procession of vehicles bump and groan up the trail. Finally, the van pulled abreast of their hiding place and roared past, followed by the two cars.

April let out a hiss of air as though she had been holding her breath. "Thank goodness," she whispered, though she must have known none of the occupants of the vehicles could possibly hear her now. "Did you see Willis and Harmon?"

Tyler nodded. "Willis is driving the van, and Harmon's in the front passenger seat of the second car."

"And I recognized one of the men in the last car. He's the same one who gave me the bluleprints to deliver to you. I think he said his name is Jim. Jim something that starts with an `S'. Stole, or maybe Stolz—something like that."

"I know one of the others, too," Tyler said grimly. "Smith. The bastard. He's who I think is behind all of this. He's riding in the back seat behind Harmon."

"They'll be out of sight as soon as they go around that curve."

Tyler's body felt cramped and restless from crouching in enforced immobility under the hemlock for so long. A need for action teased at his muscles. He tensed. "Get ready to move. We'll hightail it out of here as soon as they're gone. There's no way to tell when they'll come back down."

April started to crawl toward the trail. "Maybe we can get to a main road with some traffic before they're back."

She had just reached the perimeter of the tree branches they were hiding under, when the last car stopped.

She froze. "Oh no," she groaned. "Do you think they saw me?"

"I don't know. Just don't move."

Fear sent ice daggers through Tyler's heart. If the thugs had detected their presence, how could he protect April? He'd counted nine men as they passed, and he didn't have any kind of weapon other than a stick to defend her.

Three men got out of the Lexus and slammed the doors shut. They walked back down the trail toward the tree where April and Tyler were hiding.

Tyler picked up a knobby length of dried branch. He swallowed hard. It wasn't much, but it was all he had.

One of the men veered off into the undergrowth across the trail and concealed himself behind a bush. Tyler let out a breath of relief. He had a fair idea of what that man was doing. He could cross off one enemy for the moment.

One of the two men who stayed on the trail took a package of cigarettes from his shirt pocket, sat down on a log and lit up. The other man lounged casually at his side, occasionally glancing at the lone man remaining in the Lexus. Clearly, they hadn't detected April and Tyler's presence.

Even though they were a good seventy-five feet away, the combination of wind and peculiar mountain acoustics carried snatches of their conversation to him.

"... think we'll find Nielsen and the girl?" the man with the cigarette said.

"Who knows? Willis is full of it," the other replied.

The man took a deep drag of smoke and coughed. He spit in the general direction of his companion's feet. "The joke'll be on him, if he's lying."

"Yeah. The boss was going to get rid of him anyway, and now he's leading us to the perfect place to toss his stinking carcass."

Both men laughed harshly. The other man came out from behind the bushes. He gestured toward the car. "How's Stolz doing?"

"Not moving a muscle."

"Yeah, he's too scared to move."

The men laughed again, then the three of them went back to the Lexus. They got in, the motor started and the car disappeared around the curve.

"I wonder how Smith caught up with Willis and Harmon," Tyler said. "They were planning on leaving Seattle right away. It didn't sound like there was much chance of their changing their minds and going back to report to Smith."

He pulled himself from his prone position, sat up and speculated further. "Maybe my car tripped them up. Smith might have known whomever they use to get rid of stolen cars and had someone watch for them there. Though how he knew they had my car or me in the first place, I can't imagine. He's too clever by half to suit me."

April sat up and faced him. She turned herself into a tight little ball by hugging her legs to her chest and dropping her head to her knees. "Did you hear what they said?" she asked in a small muffled voice.

He nodded. "Let's go. We've got to get out of here fast."

Her head shot up. "We can't."

He was worried about her and didn't want to frighten her any more than she already was, but he couldn't keep the irritation out of his voice. "What do you mean 'we can't'? Have you hurt yourself?" he asked sharply.

She shook her head. "No. I'm okay. It's Willis and Harmon. Don't you understand? They're going to kill them. And I think that man Stolz is in danger, too."

"So?" he said coldly.

Her eyes widened then narrowed, and her mouth tightened. She looked at him as though he were a slug she'd scraped off the bottom of her shoe. "If you think I'm going to just run away and let two men be murdered, you're very much mistaken."

It was an effort to control his voice. "April, be reasonable. They want to murder us, too. We don't have any weapons, and Smith's men are all sure to be armed. The best way we can help Willis and Harmon and Stolz is to get out of here and find the police."

She drew herself up, her head held belligerently high, and said huffily, "Well, I'm not a reasonable woman, as you've taken great pains to point out. And I'm not going to run away and let them die. You know very well we won't be able to get the police up here before they're dead."

His control snapped. "I don't give a tinker's damn about what happens to those goons. It's you I care about, and I want you to go now!" he roared.

She thrust her head forward until they were almost nose-to-nose. "I won't."

He screwed his eyes shut and signed in exasperation. She was undoubtedly the most stubborn, most foolhardy woman there ever was. "If I promise to try to help them, will you go?"

"No."

That hurt. She didn't trust him. Not that she had any reason to take his word. Shame engulfed him. He had taken advantage of her. Why should she accept his promise?

Suddenly, it was of great importance that she believe in him. He reached out and took her hand. It was clear she only reluctantly let him hold it. "Can't you take my word for it? I'll do what I say."

Her face seemed to soften. She smiled at him. "I know you will, Tyler. It's not that. I just can't let you face them alone."

"They're terrible men, April—thieves, kidnappers, probably even murderers. Why do we have to risk our necks to save them, especially when we don't even know if we can help them anyway?"

She pulled her hand away from him. She spoke earnestly. "They're not all bad. They left us locked up in the cabin, but they could have killed us then if they'd wanted to. And Harmon even tried to leave us some food."

She paused, seemingly searching for the words to convince him. "But that's not really the point. Even if they didn't have a shred of good in them, they're still human beings. And we don't have the right to decide to let them die if there's any chance at all we can save them."

He dropped his gaze, no longer able to meet her clear-sighted intensity. He wanted to pick her up, sling her over his shoulder and carry her away down the mountain to safety, but damned if he couldn't see her point. She was right, though he hated to admit it.

"How fast can you go on that bike?" he asked.

She was quick; he had to give her that. She didn't even blink at the non sequitur. "Over fifty miles per hour on a downhill paved street without any traffic in the way."

She paused and pursed her lips. "But if you mean here, I'm not sure. The terrain isn't consistent. The road is fairly smooth in a few stretches, then there are rough patches with tree branches and rocks and holes. Why?"

"I'll try to help them though I'm not very optimistic about our chances, but you have to promise, if Smith gets on to us, you'll use that bike to get away as fast as you can. Agreed?"

She frowned at him stubbornly but finally, obviously reluctantly, nodded her head. He wished he could feel some satisfaction over the small success, but he knew it was an empty victory.

"You know," he said quietly but with deadly earnestness, "you just might be able to escape from the cars, but there's no way you can outrun a bullet."

He saw her swallow hard, before she nodded her head again.

He felt a tightness in his own throat as he watched her conquer her fear. He reached out to tuck one of her unruly curls behind her ear and leaned forward to graze her forehead with his lips. He was relieved, when she accepted the small intimacy. Just a few hours before, they had been as close as two people could be, and now there was a huge, unbridgeable gulf between them.

He tried to put all he was feeling, but didn't know how to say, into that brief kiss. "All right, then. It's all settled," he said with false heartiness. "Let's go."

He crawled out from under the branches, walked to the trail and brushed himself off, while April went after her bike. "We should stay on the road for a while," he said. "It's a risk. We don't know where they might post lookouts or where the trail comes into view, but it would take us forever to get back to the cabin, if we go the whole way through the woods."

April agreed. They made their way along the very edge of the road, taking advantage of the cover provided by overhanging tree branches.

A few wildflowers were already beginning to poke up through the old leaves lining the woodland path. Clusters of drooping red flowers on small trees stood out against the much-larger dark conifers. Bird song filled the air.

His father had loved birds and often pointed out and named different kinds for him, when he was small. He wondered what birds were making the sounds he heard now. Winter wrens? Nuthatches, thrushes, warblers?

The path he and April walked on wound through a wonderland of beauty. Grimly, he shook his head in angry denial at the ironic position in which he had somehow managed to get himself entangled. The very same path could be leading them to their deaths.

When they came to the last few curves leading to the cabin, April began to edge into the woods. "Let's hide now," she said, her voice high with nerves.

She concealed her bike under a bush near the trail, piling broken branches over it to make sure it wouldn't be seen.

They approached the area cautiously, slipping from tree to tree. Tyler dropped to the ground and motioned for April to take cover when he caught his first glimpse of the cabin. The men were milling around outside it. Some of them were carrying shovels and picks.

"What are they doing?" April whispered into his ear.

He shrugged to indicate he didn't know. He pointed at Harmon and Willis. They looked nervous. Nervous and probably panicky.

Willis couldn't seem to hold still. He ran his hands over his short-cropped hair, dropped them to adjust his jacket over his skinny shoulders, tucked his shirt into his pants, took out a cigarette, put it between his lips, then dropped it and fiercely ground it into the dirt with his shoe without ever lighting it.

Harmon seemed just as worried. His big head was lowered and swung in short arcs on his thick neck and powerful shoulders as he glanced at first one man then another like a bull penned in the corner of a corral, trying to decide whom to gore first.

April pointed to a man wearing a Mariners windbreaker. "That's the one who gave me the blueprints," she whispered. "The man in the baseball jacket."

Smith came out of the cabin. No tension pulled at his face. He looked around at the men, took a pickax from one of them and almost playfully hefted it above his head. A flicker of a smile teased the corners of his lips, when his gaze swept across Willis and Harmon. "All right, Willis, show us where you buried them," he said.

Willis flinched. He took a few steps toward the rise leading up behind the cabin, paused, turned to his right, took a couple of steps that way, then swung around to face the assembled men again.

"I ain't sure. I mean... it was dark, you know. I can't tell," Willis stammered nervously. He waved his arm wildly to encompass the forest. "Look at all them trees. Them damn trees all look alike."

Smith leaned forward and rested his weight on the pick. He looked at Harmon and spoke indulgently. "Perhaps you remember which way you went? Do you know where they're buried, Harmon?"

Harmon's beefy face turned a mottled scarlet. He struggled for words but apparently couldn't find any.

"Who's buried?" April puzzled, her brow wrinkled in concern.

Tyler thought he knew, but he didn't want to risk an answer. Their position was precarious enough without carrying on a conversation that might bring their location to the attention of one of the thugs. He held one finger to his lips to shush April then pointed at Willis, who looked like he was trying to melt away into the forest, while the men were concentrating on Harmon.

But Smith made a casual gesture toward Willis without even turning toward him, and five men instantly surrounded him. "Did you find the way?" Smith asked.

"Yeah," Willis responded glumly, his shoulders hunched and sagging halfway to the ground.

The whole group trailed after Willis. When the last man disappeared into the trees, April turned anxiously to Tyler. "What's going on? Have they really buried someone out there?"

"I'm not sure, but I think the only burial is going to be of Willis and Harmon. They're going to dig their own graves."

April's eyes widened. She hugged herself as though she were cold. The sun had disappeared once more behind a thick, dark blanket of clouds, but he didn't think the gesture had anything to do with the weather. "That's awful," she said in a strangled voice. "What are we going to do?"

It warmed him to think she was so sure he could find a solution, but it made it that much harder to admit he didn't have a clue. He rubbed his hand slowly across his face, thinking. "There are so many of them, April. I don't see how we can get Harmon and Willis away from them."

April's eyes lit up. She pulled herself into a tightly coiled crouch as though she were going to explode out of their concealing bushes. She seemed to vibrate with energy. "What we need is a diversion. Like in the movies. Then Harmon and Willis could run away."

He put a restraining hand on her shoulder. "Whoa. Stop. If you mean diversion as in you're going to distract them by letting Smith know you're here, you can forget it right now. I'm not going to let you sacrifice yourself to save those worthless thugs."

She shrugged his hand off impatiently. "Don't be silly. I'm not going to sacrifice myself." A brief shudder shook her slender body. "I don't even want to think of what Smith would do if he caught us. He's creepy."

"At least you've got that right," Tyler muttered.

"Come on. They're getting too far ahead of us. We'll think of something. A safe distraction."

She darted from tree to tree, following the men. Tyler followed reluctantly. How had he ever let her talk him into this impossibly noble, utterly asinine scheme? His own unguarded car and a route to safety were only a few hundred feet away. He could easily disable the other two vehicles, and even if there were no keys in the Lexus, he could hot-wire the car, then he and April would be out of here.

The sound of the car's motor starting and their driving away might even provide the diversion April wanted for Willis and Harmon, but would she settle for that? Oh no, she'd never be satisfied until she could see with her own two emerald greens the men getting away. No matter how you startled Smith and his men, whether with a car motor or some other scheme, there was no predicting what the outcome would be, anyway. Were Willis and Harmon quick-witted enough to take advantage of a momentary change of focus of their captors? Willis maybe, but he wouldn't want to put odds on Harmon's ability to respond instantly to a fleeting opportunity.

But could he really live with two murders on his conscience, knowing he hadn't done everything he could to help?

He didn't think so. Leaving Willis and Harmon to die would have nagged at him for the rest of his life.

April seemed to know him better than he knew himself. He didn't like that. He didn't like it one little bit.

He sighed and tried to emulate April's seemingly effortless, quiet stealth through the forest. He watched her glide silently through the ferns, as graceful and lovely as a doe. She had a knack for luring him into situations, where he didn't want to be. Even now it was hard for him to believe they had actually made love.

Could a man have sex against his will? He pushed a branch out of his way and snorted at such a ludicrous idea. He had wanted her with every fiber of his being. It was just before and after the act that he was opposed to the idea.

He tried to harden his heart against her. He was fairly sure making love had been as explosive and life altering for her as it had been for him. But she would get over it.

He savagely kicked at a sword fern in his path. But would he ever get over it? That was the problem. Even now, in the middle of a ludicrous rescue attempt, he wanted her. It consumed his reason; it clouded his judgment, it seemed to take him over.

He halted and closed his eyes briefly, trying to regain control. He would get them out of here, he vowed fervently, get both of them out now. Once he was away from this fireball masquerading as a woman, he would be okay. He could leave behind in the wilderness all the dangerous thoughts and feelings she stirred up. When he got home to his real life, he would be back on track.

He gritted his teeth then sprinted to catch up with her. He only had to hold on a little longer. He'd think of something to save Willis and Harmon, then he'd be safe. And he didn't mean from Smith and his gang. Much more important, he'd be safely away from his consuming need for April.

As he rounded a nursery stump, he caught a glimpse of one of her battered shoes as it disappeared under a spreading hemlock. She was crawling on the ground now. He heard voices and the harsh sounds of a pick and a shovel scraping against rock. He dropped to the ground himself and inched under the tree after April.

He crawled up next to her. She'd picked a ringside seat for the proceedings. She was close to the men. Much too close. He swore under his breath.

Several of the men, including Willis and Harmon, were digging near the base of an outcropping of naked rock. The other men were gathered around in a loose circle, watching. Several downed trees leaned at precarious angles against the bare cliff.

In spite of the recent rains that softened the ground, the men were digging in a rocky area, and their progress was slow. The diameter of the hole they had dug was wide but not very deep yet.

"You picked a hell of a place to bury anybody, Willis," a heavy-set man, who was sweating profusely, growled.

"Yes, Willis," Smith said. "Are you certain this is the location? The soil doesn't seem to be very loose. We could look some more just to be sure." Tyler thought he heard a kind of ghoulish humor in his voice.

"This is the spot," Willis responded glumly, then grunted as he threw a large rock out of the hole.

"It was quite unfortunate you weren't able to follow my directions and intercept the blueprints, but I suppose once Nielsen saw the specs, getting rid of him and the courier was the next best recourse," Smith said.

April turned to Tyler, her mouth open and her eyes wide with shock. He understood that she had just realized who was supposed to be buried under the stones.

"So, if I done such a good job, why do we hafta dig 'em up? We'll just hafta plant 'em all over again," Willis whined.

"Oh, I think you know the answer to that," Smith said, smiling paternally.

In spite of the danger April was apparently too astounded to keep quiet. "It's just like Tom Sawyer and Huckleberry Finn."

Tyler frowned at her, but she continued to whisper anyway, evidently thinking he hadn't understood her reference to the book.

"You know, when everybody thought Tom and Huck had drowned, and they snuck back to watch the ceremony for themselves at the church."

She paused. Her face looked pinched and pale in the filtered light that flickered through the hemlock boughs. Her voice was thready and faint when she continued. "I have this terrible feeling we're attending our own funerals."

Eight

The men dug deeper and deeper into the rocky soil. One by one, all but Willis and Harmon climbed out of the hole. Now the two of them stood almost chest-deep in the excavation. April figured she and Tyler didn't have much time left to decide what to do.

"You made certain no one would ever find the bodies, didn't you, boys?" Smith said. He behaved like a cat toying with a mouse. He practically purred with satisfaction. His voice might sound velvety, but April knew it only hid the sharp claws under his smooth surface.

The men standing around the hole no longer chuckled at Smith's comments. Everyone above ground, except for Smith, radiated a certain tense expectancy.

"Buried them deep," he continued. "An excellent idea. I agree wholeheartedly. It's always been one of my guiding principles."

Willis looked as though he might be sick at any moment. A slick of clammy perspiration coated his pasty-gray face, and his eyes darted so frantically from side to side, it almost seemed as though they would fly from their sockets.

Harmon, on the other hand, seemed oblivious to his surroundings. He kept digging like an automaton, his head down, not looking at anyone. His powerful arms seemed joined to his shovel as he threw up a continuous stream of dirt and rocks to form a towering pile of rubble beside the hole.

Just listening to Smith caused a bitter taste to rise into April's throat. She tried to swallow it away. What a disgusting man. He seemed to be enjoying himself, as though this whole production was an entertainment put on especially for him.

It was hard for her to believe such people really existed. Here was a man who cared nothing for human life. He was perfectly willing to risk the lives of innocent bystanders in his unsafe buildings just to fill his pockets. When the roof came crashing down, it didn't matter to him who was crushed, young or old. April shuddered at the thought. They had to find a way to keep that from happening. First save Willis and Harmon, then bring Smith to justice.

She started when Tyler tapped her on the shoulder. He slid back low on his hands and knees toward the other side of the hemlock under which they were hiding. He beckoned for her to follow him.

Did he have a plan? She hoped he did, because she had absolutely no idea of what to do. She hated to admit it, but the situation looked utterly hopeless. The sick feeling in her stomach told her they were going to have to stand by helplessly and watch while Smith and his men shot Willis and Harmon down in the hole like vermin in a well.

After they crawled out from under the tree, Tyler pulled her close to him and put his mouth to her ear. Strange, in spite of all her fear and worry, his lips felt wonderfully warm and sensual. April wished with all her heart they were somewhere safe and private where she didn't have to think of anything but the lovely sensation of his mouth and breath caressing every whorl and spiral of her ear.

He said the same thing she had been thinking. "We have to move now, April. Do you see that little dam the broken tree branches make against the cliff? Where all the rocks are piled?"

He pointed at the wall of stone behind the hole the men had dug. She sighted along the line his finger indicated and saw a long, thin tree trunk leaning against the cliff, with several smaller branches wedged between the tree and the rock. Pebbles and small rocks had accumulated there, supported by a latticework of branches.

She nodded her head, and he whispered in her ear again. "I'm going to throw a rock at the branches. If I do it right, it should cause quite an avalanche. Hopefully, they'll think someone dislodged a stone from above the cliff and head that way."

She felt his lips form a little smile against her ear. "It's the diversion you wanted."

Then his voice turned grim again. "It's not much of a plan. We don't have any way to warn Willis and Harmon, so they'll be ready to run, but Willis, at least, looks like he's about ready to bolt anyway, so maybe if the other men are distracted, even for just a few moments, it'll give him the edge he needs to get away."

He moved away briefly and rubbed his hand over his face in a worried gesture. Then, almost roughly, he pulled her close to him. "I don't know about Harmon. He's not too swift. But it's the best I can come up with."

It might work, April thought. And anyway, she didn't have a better idea. With time running out, it would have to do. It was the only plan they had.

He gripped her to him fiercely. "And I don't know about us, either. If anyone notices the direction the rock came from, they could be right on us. I want you to start moving down the mountain now, away from the road, before I make my move. I think Willis and Harmon will head for the cars, with Smith's men after them. So, we're going the other way. And we're not waiting to see if they get away. We're doing the best we can for them, then we're going to save ourselves. Understand?"

April nodded. Then, impulsively, she whipped her head around, so that instead of pressing his lips against her ear, Tyler's mouth was suddenly flush against her own.

She knew he didn't want her to play any role in his future. He wouldn't or couldn't reciprocate the feelings she had for him. The pain from his rejection was devastating, but she still wanted one more kiss. They might die in a few moments. And even if they did manage to get to safety, they almost certainly would never see one another again. She wanted one last moment with him. One last goodbye.

She kept her eyes open. When their lips touched, first she saw surprise register in his eyes. Then they flared into passion. His arms encircled her. He pulled her so closely to him they seemed to meld into one, then the strength of his embrace lifted her from her feet. They clung together with an intensity that made the forest and the danger disappear.

Finally, Tyler loosened his hold on her. He pulled his head away from hers and let her slowly slide down his body. Once her feet were on the ground, he released her. It had been exactly the grand farewell she had wanted. He might not choose to allow her into his life if they ever got home, but she had made sure he would never forget her. She'd be willing to bet on that.

He took one last deep breath, and a lopsided grin crooked his mouth. He gestured toward Smith. She raised her head and straightened her shoulders, tense and alert. She was ready now.

Swiftly, she moved down the mountain, away from Smith and his men. Out of the corner of her eye, she noted Tyler watching her, checking to see if she was following his instructions. When she had put a distance between them, the minute he turned his back to her, April stopped so she could see what was going to happen.

She watched Tyler scout the ground. He picked up and hefted several stones before discarding them. Once he found exactly the right rock, he hid behind a bush tall enough to duck below but short enough so, when standing, he would have a clear view and a clean throw.

He crouched low behind the bush. Even from her distance, April could see the tension in his body. His intensity shot an answering chord through her.

She imagined how he must feel, as he observed the scene, waiting for the perfect moment to make his desperate move. She could practically feel his muscles trembling with anxiety.

Suddenly, he leaped up from behind the bush and hurled the stone with terrific strength and speed. Then he whirled and sped down the mountain toward April. Frantically, she turned to run, too, but he caught up with her in a matter of minutes. From the furious look on his face, she guessed it hadn't taken him long to figure out she had waited for him. He grabbed her arm and dragged her along with him at a tremendous pace. His long legs seemed to fly over the ground. She would have had to possess wings to keep up with him.

A tremendous uproar had broken out back by the cliff the moment Tyler had thrown the rock. She could hear shouts and curses and the sound of running feet and bodies crashing through trees and underbrush. Fervently, she willed Harmon and Willis to safety. She wanted them in good shape, when the police picked them up for a nice long stay in jail.

A single gunshot rang out, followed by the echoing boom of a whole volley of gunfire. April leaped forward even faster, her whole body vibrating with nervous tension. She felt like a harp with a giant hand violently plucking every string at once.

Had the bullets found their mark? Had she and Tyler risked their lives for nothing? Willis and Harmon had kidnapped and threatened her. They had tied her up, frightening her and taking away her dignity and freedom, but they hadn't actually physically hurt her. She didn't want them to die.

Then she realized the bullets might be aimed at her. Terror gave her the wings she had wished for earlier. Shoulder bag banging between her shoulder blades, she flew downhill, once falling to her knees when she tripped over a tree root, but Tyler yanked her back to her feet again, and they raced on until her lungs were burning and each breath was a painful effort. She had no idea how long they had been running. It seemed like forever.

Tree branches whipped by, slapping her face and threatening decapitation. Rocks and stumps leaped into her path with astonishing speed. The decision to duck under or jump over the obstacles that appeared had to be made in seconds.

Finally, the terrors of the last twenty-four hours caught up with her. The lack of food and sleep and the roller coaster of emotional highs and lows had taken a heavier toll than she had realized. Her athlete's body, which had never failed her before, gave out.

She slid down a steep bank and collapsed at the bottom. She managed to get up, but she couldn't go on. Her thigh and calf muscles were on fire. She pushed her hand against her ribs, trying to ease the stitch in her side, and bent forward, trying to fill her lungs with air, but she could only manage shallow, rasping gasps. She sank back down to the ground.

With an easy leap, Tyler's long legs had cleared the bank that had been her undoing, but the moment he realized she had stopped, he turned back to her. "April, come on! We have to keep moving."

"I can't," she wheezed. "Go ahead. I'll catch up."

He stood watching her, towering over her, listening to her labored breathing as he caught his breath himself, his features stamped with concern.

After a few moments it dawned on April that Tyler's breathing, mingled with her own, was the only thing she did hear. No running footsteps, no crashing through the woods, no stealthy approach and, best of all, no gunshots.

As her breathing slowly returned to normal and she could listen better, she strained her ears. Perhaps she caught a distant sound of a motor, but that was all.

Tyler was breathing hard, too, but he didn't sound as bad as she did. *Pretty good for a businessman,* she thought wryly. *He must do some kind of exercise to stay so fit.*

"Do you think they're coming after us?" she asked.

"Impossible to say, but I think we're okay for the moment. If some of them are following us, we must have left them pretty far behind."

He was clearly anxious to move on. His eyes were never still as he scanned their surroundings.

"As far as I could tell, they all ran toward the cars. But I don't know what happened after that. We can rest for a minute, but we've got to go on as soon as we can. We're not safe yet."

"Do you think Willis and Harmon are okay?"

He looked exasperated. "How the hell should I know? We're damned lucky to be in one piece ourselves. I don't intend to think about them again until I give my statement to the police."

He offered her his hand. "We've rested long enough. Let's go."

Refusing to meet his eyes, April stubbornly shook her head and remained sitting on the ground. She knew he would be angry. "I have to know. They might still need help. I'm going back to see."

He dropped his hand and stared at her incredulously, his mouth hanging open in shock. "You can't be serious."

"When you said to run away, it seemed like the right thing to do, but I was scared and not really thinking. We might have just made things worse for them. I have to find out."

"I hardly think we could have made things any worse for them." His voice was ugly with sarcasm. "If you'd use your befuddled brain, you might recall Smith was going to shoot them. I can't think of many things much worse than that."

April flushed at his harsh words, but they only stiffened her resolve. She had to know what had happened. She stood up. "I'm going back."

Tyler exploded. "What's wrong with you? Is this some kind of an adopt-a-thug mission, or what? I thought it was stupid trying to help them in the first place, but going back now is absolutely insane!"

He clamped his mouth shut as though he didn't trust what might come out next, turned his back on her and stalked a few paces into the woods before he wheeled around and returned to continue his attack. She could see him struggling to control his voice, probably not in consideration for her, but more likely because he had remembered sounds carry in the mountains, and he didn't want Smith to hear him.

"Think, April. Smith knows someone is out here now, and he probably has a pretty good idea it's us since he came up here looking for us in the first place. We might as well have put up a billboard announcing our presence."

He grabbed her arm with one hand and tipped her chin up with the other, none too gently, forcing her to look him in the eye. "He's on the alert now. It won't be so easy to sneak around and spy on them. He'll be watching for us, at the very least. And what's a whole lot more likely is that he's sent men to track us down. They're probably on their way down the mountain right now."

He dropped his hands, releasing her. She stepped away from him and rubbed her chin resentfully. Was it really only a few short hours before that his hands had been so gentle? It seemed like a thousand years ago.

His voice was calm now, quiet, controlled and distant. "What are you going to do if you stumble onto a group of three or four armed men? Men who are looking for you and plan to shoot you? What are you going to do then?"

He sounded almost as though he were posing an academic question, which, considering the subject, gave his words a bizarre twist. April felt like crying. What had happened to their sense of camaraderie? Their feeling of shared purpose? Tyler was so cold now. In spite of the sweat dripping down her forehead and trickling down her neck, she almost shivered. All of his warmth and concern had disappeared.

April looked up at the leaden sky. It was probably going to start raining again soon, she thought, trying to distract herself from her feelings and the situation. She was sweating from their mad run, but the air was cold and forbidding. She should dry off before she caught a chill from the weather, never mind the climate Tyler was generating.

She pulled out her trusty but considerably worse-for-wear bandanna and wiped her face and neck. Tyler stared at her intently. Apparently, he still expected her to go with him.

"I'm not going to change my mind, Tyler," she said as calmly as she could. It was pretty hard to appear unruffled when she knew her face must look like a beet, her hair like a haystack and her clothes like filthy rags, but she tried for unassailable confidence. "You heard the guns. Willis or Harmon might be lying up there right now, deserted and bleeding to death. I could help."

His eyes swept over her in a scathing appraisal. He clearly thought she was a moron. "You can be sure if Smith brought them down, he made certain they were dead. You can't help a dead man. They either got away, or they didn't. There isn't any in between."

Suddenly, Tyler threw back his head and laughed, a harsh, ugly, tearing sound without a snippet of real mirth. April took an involuntary step back. His laughter now was somehow more menacing than when he was yelling.

He rubbed his rough, unshaven chin in a speculative way as he squinted at her. "You know, I don't think you really give a damn about Willis and Harmon. That isn't it at all, is it?"

He stepped toward her, and again, April apprehensively moved away. "It's the thrill, isn't it? You love the excitement. You don't mind risking your neck because you think you're immortal, just like my parents. You don't believe anything could ever happen to you. You think you're above ordinary people—different, invulnerable—and damn the consequences to everyone around you!"

April's face blanched. Her whole body trembled at the force of his diatribe. She wanted to shout at him. *No! I'm not like that. You don't understand. I'm not.* But a kernel of doubt kept her silent.

Could she really be like he said? Arrogant? Flying in the face of reason? Unconscionably endangering others, even those she cared about deeply?

It was true she liked excitement. But she didn't think she usually took unnecessary risks. They were in extraordinary circumstances now, a situation most people would never have to face in a lifetime. She wanted to do the right thing.

April tipped her chin up defiantly. His attack was unfair. He might be correct that her plan to check on the men was foolish, but she knew she wasn't doing it just for a cheap thrill. And anyway, after the way he had talked to her, she refused to back down now.

She got up, her legs trembling. After pulling her jacket down and adjusting her shoulder bag, she turned to start in the direction of the cabin. Her heart sank as she thought how long and how fast they had run. It would take forever to make her way back up the mountain, and it was all uphill.

She twisted her head to look at Tyler. He wasn't moving. He stood amid the ferns, planted as solidly as one of the giant spruces around them, his arms crossed over his chest as he glowered at her.

"Are you coming?" she asked hopefully, a tremor in her voice.

"No. If you're determined to go on a suicide mission, you'll go alone. I don't want any part of it."

"Please?" It was as close to begging as she'd ever come. Now her face burned with shame and embarrassment as well as exertion.

"No. The more important issue is stopping Smith. I need to get to the authorities, so we can start checking all the buildings he's played any part in constructing. If we both die out here, he might get away with it, and who knows what kind of tragedy might happen? You'd forgotten all about that, hadn't you? You're so crazy about Willis and Harmon you're totally ignoring the bigger picture. I care a whole lot more about the people who might be in danger in one of his buildings right now than I do about those two creeps."

He looked so smug and self-righteous, that for a moment April just wanted to smack him. She had thought about the dangerous buildings. She did care about all of the other people who could get hurt. But doubt still plagued her. Maybe he was right. Maybe she did have her priorities wrong. She couldn't think of anything else to say to him to defend herself or to convince him to help her.

April turned away from Tyler and started climbing, totally demoralized, but determined to hide her uncertainty. Her legs ached and cramped; she was weak from hunger and scant sleep and trembling with anxiety. Near exhaustion, only the monumental stubbornness she was born with kept her putting one foot in front of another.

In a flash of memory she saw her mother frowning at her, the expression on her mother's face very similar to the one Tyler was sporting right now, as she reproached April for climbing up on the garage roof to rescue a baby bird that had fallen out of its nest, after she had been expressly forbidden to scale anything higher than her tricycle.

"Your stubbornness will be the death of you yet," her mother had scolded.

Her mother was almost always right. And the baby bird had still died in spite of all of April's efforts. April bit at her chapped lip and squeezed her eyes shut.

"Please, Mother," she whispered, then opened her eyes and picked up her pace, "be wrong just this once."

Nine

April felt as though she were dragging herself up the mountain. Her feet were as leaden as her heart. Her pulse throbbed dully in her throat. It beat in time with the mantra resounding in her head: *Fool, fool, fool!* Why had she insisted on going on a fool's errand?

She had been walking for about twenty minutes, questioning every step, when she heard male voices. Even as she first perceived the sound, it grew louder. The men were coming straight at her! Frantically, April searched for a place to hide.

Near her lay a fallen tree that had sprouted from a nursery stump. It had reached a good size before its roots lost their purchase in the crumbling, rotting host.

Quickly, April crept under the tip of the tree near where it touched the ground and the branches were thick and dense. It was a little like ducking under a tent flap and crawling inside.

Adjusting her shoulder bag so the long protruding tube of blueprints wouldn't poke through the foliage, she prayed whoever was coming down the mountain wouldn't see her.

She peeked through the net of branches. They were almost on top of her! Only two men. It was hard to tell who they were. She was low on the ground, looking up through thick branches. She only glimpsed bits and pieces of the men, but the one item she clearly identified gave her heart a jolt. She bit her lip when she saw the unmistakable metallic glint and shape of a revolver.

The men loomed larger into her limited field of vision. They were walking straight toward her! April tried to make herself as small as possible. Had they spotted her? Were they going to walk right up to the fallen tree and shoot her?

Her pulse rate accelerated into the three-digit range. Her chest heaved with the effort to get enough oxygen to her terror-depleted lungs. The sounds of her breathing and heartbeat roared in her ears. Could they hear it? Was that how they had found her?

She wished Tyler were with her. Funny how much more frightened she felt now that she was alone than when she had been with him. How could she have grown dependent on him so quickly?

She shivered. He couldn't have possibly made it any clearer just how much he didn't want to be with her. He had abandoned her. But she'd been in tight places before, dozens of times in fact, and managed just fine without him or anyone else, thank you very much. She could handle this situation by herself, too. She was sure she could.

The footsteps came closer. Dead leaves swirled around their shoes with a cacophonous crunching. A rain-scented breeze stirred the branches all around her, raising giant goose bumps on her sweat-drenched skin. She flushed cold then hot. Every bit of sensory input was magnified a thousand times.

She felt like a trapped rabbit huddled under the tree. She couldn't stay there another second. She scanned the surrounding terrain wildly, preparing to bolt.

She would zigzag. Wasn't that what you were supposed to do, when someone was shooting at you? So the target was always changing, not moving in a straight line?

She had just started to move when she heard a thump right next to her. Startled, she swung her head around and saw camel's-hair cloth poking through the veil of evergreen needles that hid her. She knew for sure the identity of one of the men now. Smith. She began to shake silently. He was the only one of the band of men wearing a camel's-hair greatcoat.

He was sitting close by on a log that lay parallel to and on top of some of the branches of the tree she was hiding under, sitting with his back to her. With a rush of relief, she realized he hadn't seen her. She took a long, slow, deep breath as quietly as she could, trying to calm her nerves. She was safe, at least for the moment.

Smith was talking to the man who had come with him, but April had been too panic-stricken to hear a single word. Now that she knew they hadn't discovered her presence, she tried to focus enough to listen.

"Well, Stolz," Smith said easily, settling himself more comfortably on the log, "it's about time we balanced a few accounts."

"I thought you wanted to look for Nielsen and the courier," Stolz replied. "Appears you're right. They must have caused the fiasco with Willis and Harmon at the, uh... grave... back there. Somebody went through here not long ago, and it looks like they were in a hell of a hurry. They can't keep up that kind of pace for long. If we go on after them, we ought to catch up soon."

"In due course, Stolz, in due course. Nielsen's time is coming, but first you need to come up with some answers. Tell me about the blueprints."

April could see Stolz's feet, as he began to inch away from the log where Smith was sitting toward the big trees at the edge of the little clearing.

"I don't know what you mean," Stolz said. "I just packaged them for delivery the way you told me."

Smith slowly swung the gun, tracking Stolz's snail-like retreat, until the revolver was less than a foot from April. He shifted his weight on the log, causing a shower of dead pine needles to rain down on her face.

"But the set of blueprints you packaged weren't the same ones you'd been working on that day," Smith said. "Now how do you suppose that could have happened?"

April saw his finger just perceptibly tighten on the trigger of the revolver. She felt as though she were frozen in a moment of time where she had to make a life or death decision. If she didn't act quickly, something dreadful was going to happen.

Gathering all her courage, she lunged forward through the branches and grabbed the gun from behind, tearing it out of Smith's grasp. Her momentum catapulted her over the log so that she somersaulted into the clearing where she landed in a heap between the two men. Chest heaving, she scrambled to her feet, pointing the gun first at one man, then the other. Both started back.

Every muscle in her body was trembling, even her cheeks were quivering, but she tried to adopt a strong, aggressive posture as though she knew all about guns and was totally in control of the situation. Too bad she'd never touched a real revolver before in her life. It was as repugnant to her as if she were hoisting a stiff dead rat.

"What the hell... ?" Smith cried, teetering on the log he was sitting on, clutching at the rough bark to keep from toppling backwards into the branches from where April had just sprung. His voice was almost a shriek; he had finally lost the creamy, amused tone he had used when he'd been toying with Willis and Harmon. And April had the satisfaction of watching the smug expression, the very same expression that had continuously adorned his face since she had first seen him, dissolve into apprehension and fear.

But then it was April's turn to be startled. She almost jumped out of her skin at the sound of applause coming from the clearing's edge.

Clapping his hands as he walked toward her, Tyler emerged from amongst the trees. "Well done, April. You're astounding."

"Tyler!" April gasped. He'd come back for her after all! He hadn't deserted her. He did care about her. He must.

"I'd be careful of him if I were you, Missy," Smith said calmly as he slowly pushed himself to an upright position on the log. Casually, he rubbed his hands together to rid them of clinging bits of bark, apparently recovering his equanimity along with his equilibrium. "Nielsen and Stolz make quite a pair. I've been in the building game a long time—thought I'd seen every scam invented—but they still fooled me."

"What are you talking about?" April asked scornfully. "Tyler doesn't even know Mr. Stolz."

Her voice changed, losing just a shade of confidence. She stepped back so she could see Tyler's face. "You don't, do you?"

The three men were all about an equal distance from her now. The heavy gun pulled at her hands, coaxing them toward the ground. She tightened her grip.

"You know I don't." Tyler didn't even bother to look at her. A reassuring glance would have been welcome, but he was staring speculatively at Stolz. "I can't figure out your motivation. Why did you send me that particular set of blueprints? It can't have been an accident."

Stolz's gaze shifted uneasily from the gun in April's hand to Smith and back to Tyler. He shrugged. "I don't suppose there's anything to gain by keeping it a secret any longer. My cover's blown anyway."

He paused, took a deep breath then exhaled shakily. "It started with my nephew. He was only four years old, my baby sister's son, and now, because of him," he pointed at Smith, his eyes glaring, his face contorted with hatred, "he's dead!"

The awful word shot out with explosive force, as Stolz took what looked like an involuntary step toward Smith, his accusing, pointing finger slowly curling into a rigid clenched fist.

The man's thin body trembled. He swallowed hard as he lowered his hand, apparently trying to get himself under control, but his voice still sounded clogged when he continued.

"My sister and her family were at her older son's track meet. The bleachers collapsed. A lot of people were hurt, but little Jeffie was the only one who died. He was crushed. 'A freak accident,' the officials said."

April felt sick. She could imagine all too well the terrible scene—excited, cheering children and parents turned in an instant into moaning victims.

"But I knew it wasn't an accident," Stolz grated out. "I found out who built the stadium. It was Smith's company, of course. One of his early, smaller projects. I was sure it was all due to shoddy construction, but I needed proof."

"And you found it," Tyler said quietly. "Two sets of blueprints. But why did you send the substandard set to me?"

Stolz turned to Tyler. "I was ready to go to the authorities. I had all the hard evidence I needed, but first I wanted to know if you were involved. I figured if I sent the secret spec sheets to you and nothing happened—you didn't say or do anything—well, that would prove you and Smith were working together and that you'd known all along Smith never planned to follow the official bid when his crew did the actual construction."

"And what if I was innocent?" Tyler bit off the words angrily. "Did it ever cross your mind Smith might retaliate? And how would you know for sure whether I did or didn't confront Smith? Surely, you aren't aware of all of his conversations, of everything that goes on in his office."

Stolz looked at the ground. He rubbed one thumb over the back of his hand as though he were trying to scrub away a dirty spot. "I didn't think it through. I just wanted to know if you were involved. I didn't even plan it. Smith told me to get the final plans ready for the courier to deliver to you. I wasn't even supposed to know about the defective set, I'd always worked on the official blueprints, but I knew where they were. I just bundled them up and handed them over to the courier."

He looked up apologetically at April. "I'm sorry. I certainly never intended for you to get hurt. I never dreamed they'd kidnap you."

He looked back at Tyler and squared his shoulders. "I suppose I was hoping you'd take care of Smith. After you'd contacted the authorities, I would have backed you up, of course; but if you had been the one to take the initiative, it would have been a whole lot safer for me. I'm really sorry all this happened to you. I can see now you don't have anything to do with it. I should have left you out of the whole thing."

Tyler walked over and clasped one of Stolz's shoulders. He spoke quietly but with fierce intensity. "The hell I don't have anything to do with it. It's my name and reputation on the line. You've shown real courage and resourcefulness, man. You don't have anything to apologize for. I should be thanking you. If unsafe buildings had gone up and someone had gotten hurt, I'd never have forgiven myself."

"Well, well," Smith said laconically. "They make quite a pair, don't they? Teamed up against evil old me."

His voice deepened and took on authority and weight. His eyes bored into April's. "Too bad there's not a word of truth in it. They're putting on quite an act for you, young lady, seeing as how you're holding the gun. If they dreamed up that story on the spot to convince you to hand over the gun, I must give them credit for remarkable extemporaneous abilities, but more than likely they'd perfected a cover story a long time ago to fall back on if they ever got caught. A cover to put the blame on me for their scheming."

"What scheming?" April puzzled. *Whatever is he talking about?*

"They've been working together all along, of course. Who knows how many innocent contractors they've fooled? I figure it goes something like this: Nielsen Development gets a legitimate bid from a contractor for a project, then Stolz worms his way into the organization and, after all the architectural plans are supposedly finalized, substitutes bad blueprints for the real ones."

April felt confused. *None of this wild tale can possibly be true, can it? Building doesn't work that way, does it?* And what about the men's discussion she and Tyler had overheard along the road? She couldn't have misunderstood the whole conversation, could she? Surely, Smith was just a crook trying to save his own skin. But what did she really know about anyone here? She'd stumbled into something she knew very little about.

She racked her brain, trying to remember everything that had happened, everything that had been said. What incriminating evidence—real facts—did she know that pinpointed who was behind all of this? She knew who had kidnapped her but not, for sure, the why.

She flushed hotly. Even Tyler, whom she'd given everything to, what did she really know about him? Only what he had told her. She felt like she'd been with him for an eternity, but as impossible as it was to believe, it had actually been less than twenty-four hours.

There could really be no doubt Smith was a criminal. The bits of conversation she had heard between Willis and Harmon at the cabin—they had said they worked for Smith and that their goal was to recover the incriminating blueprints for him—the conversation between the two men along the roadway about the boss planning to get rid of Willis, and Smith's own words to Willis and Harmon while they dug in the forest about how he was glad they'd buried the bodies deep—all clearly and indisputably indicted Smith.

But was it possible that at some earlier point Smith and Tyler had collaborated? That later there had been a falling out among thieves? Why, then, would Smith have bothered to send Willis and Harmon after the blueprints, if Tyler had already known there were two sets? Maybe the spec sheets were too incriminating to take a chance on someone other than Tyler opening the package when it arrived at his office.

Perhaps Tyler had come after her after he had seen the shoddy blueprints so he could find out who had sent them and why and eliminate that person to protect his own interests. Smith probably didn't confide in Willis, Harmon or Stolz; none of them might have known that Tyler had been working with Smith all along.

Stolz might not be telling the truth now, either. Maybe the whole thing had been a gigantic blunder; he had sent the wrong blueprints by accident, and he had just made up the heart-rending story about his nephew on the spot, thinking Tyler was a legitimate businessman who would speak up for him if the law became involved, so he could just conveniently disappear after he was out of Smith's clutches.

Perhaps once Smith saw his scheme with Tyler falling apart, he decided to take advantage of Tyler's accidental kidnapping to get rid of him along with Stolz and April and Willis and Harmon all at the same time.

Perhaps they were all colossal liars...

Some of her confusion must have shown on her face, because Tyler stared at her sharply. "April... " he said, with a question in his voice, as he took a step toward her.

Without conscious thought on her part, almost as though the gun had a mind of its own, she swung it in Tyler's direction, until it was pointing directly at him.

He froze, looking as stunned as if she'd actually shot him. He spoke to Smith through rigid lips while continuing to stare at April. "If you're such an innocent, why did you send thugs after April?"

Smith pursed his thin lips as though he'd bitten into something distasteful. "It was a terrible mistake. When I began to suspect something wasn't on the up and up with your company, I made some discreet inquiries, trying to find someone who could investigate for me. Apparently the people who do that kind of work are often only a step above the criminal element themselves, but what could I do?"

He shrugged helplessly. "I had to protect myself. I hired Harmon and Willis to gather evidence against you, Nielsen, but I had no idea their methods would be so crude."

His thin lips smiled ingratiatingly at April. "Believe me, if I'd known they'd do anything so outrageous as involve an innocent bystander such as yourself, I never would have employed their services, no matter what the ultimate damage might have been to me and my company."

April's stomach fairly turned at the slick, unctuous, self-serving words. Surely her instincts were correct about Tyler? He was innocent, wasn't he? Evil seemed to coil up from Smith like steam from a boiling pot. But was she fooling herself into believing there could be no possible involvement with Smith because she was attracted to Tyler?

She examined the three men. Smith was a study in brown: his hair faded almost to tan, his eyes a bleached mahogany, grainy beige skin, pigskin gloves and the all-enveloping camel's-hair coat. He looked like a pile of dead leaves amongst all the evergreens.

Small, thin, hunched into his baseball jacket, Stolz wavered from one foot to another. Could he really be brave and clever enough to risk his own safety seeking justice for his nephew? Or bad enough to join forces with Tyler to use Smith's company for their own ends? Or was he more likely just a cowardly man trying to cover-up for a foolish mistake?

And then there was Tyler. Tall, lean, handsome, with soulful dark eyes and enough sex appeal for ten men, he had totally convinced her of his dedication to strengthening the community with his tales of lost parents and family-friendly buildings, but what real evidence did she have regarding his character? Was she so sexually naïve that an attractive man could convince her he was entirely different than his true nature? Was she merely hearing and seeing in Tyler what she wanted to see? Perhaps he was one of those men who, as a matter of course, made up a whole false persona to seduce whatever woman they were interested in for the moment.

It's all such a muddle. Is anyone telling the truth?

She had been so stressed, mentally and physically, by her ordeal, it was no wonder she might have trouble trusting her senses and her memory. She hated to admit to any weakness, but it was a wonder she could still stand, much less decide what to do. She needed to make a plan. It was always better to take action than to stand around dithering over the possibilities.

Maybe she should use the gun to herd all three of them to the van, make one of them tie the others up, tie the last one up herself then drive all of them to a police station and let the authorities sort out the truth. Except, she was forgetting Smith's other men could be anywhere between here and the cabin. What to do? She felt so alone.

Tyler took a step toward her. She held the gun steady, pointed directly at his chest. Of course she had believed they were both victims when they were tied up together, who wouldn't? But it really wasn't proof of anything. She wanted to trust him—he had stolen her heart even if he had never stolen anything else—but what if she was wrong?

"Don't come any closer, Tyler," she said warningly, but he didn't even pause. He was almost upon her. She felt panicky. Could she really pull the trigger? Would the gun even go off if she did? She had to decide, now!

Out of the corner of her eye, she caught a blur of brown. Tyler had distracted her attention from Smith. Now Smith chopped the edge of his palm down hard on her wrist. Her fingers went numb. She tried desperately to hang on to the gun, but it flew up in a high arc, as her arm went down. It disappeared into a tangle of brambles and dead leaves.

In an instant Stolz and Smith had thrown themselves into the briars and were wrestling with one another and the thorns. Tyler went after them.

April watched in horror. What had she done? She'd had the upper hand, and she'd lost it, and she still had no idea whom to trust.

As she observed in dismay the two men tumbling through the bushes, the gun discharged. A piece of bark flew from a nearby tree and hit her cheek with stinging impact. She cried out.

Tyler had almost reached the brambles, but at the sound of April's shriek he turned back toward her.

April put her hand to her cheek. It hurt ferociously. She pulled her hand away and saw blood drip from her fingers to the forest floor.

Her head whirled with confusion and pain. She'd accomplished nothing here and very likely made things much worse for whoever was innocent. She didn't know how or whom to help. The only thing she could think to do now was save herself.

She spun away from the thrashing, cursing chaos in the berry bushes and sprinted toward the cover of the trees at the edge of the clearing.

"April, wait!" Tyler called after her.

For just an instant her step faltered. She wanted to believe in him, she wanted him, so much! Her muscles, her heart, the very fiber of her being screamed at her to go back. They remembered his gentle caresses and the strength of his embrace.

But she couldn't trust Tyler even if she loved him. Her heart might be wrong. If he really was the mastermind behind the resort construction scheme, he might very well murder Smith to shut him up and perhaps her, too.

Tyler had said she was the wrong woman for him. Maybe it was because he truly was a criminal.

She had to keep going; she had to get away and find the police. They could figure it all out. She prayed Tyler was all she had believed him to be, but she didn't dare to stick around to find out. Her emotions clouded rational thought. She simply couldn't figure out who was right and who was in the wrong.

April darted through the trees, her eyes skimming the terrain, searching for a clear path through the thick undergrowth. Tears stung at her eyes and blurred her vision. She blundered into a dense thicket of salmonberry that snagged her jacket. Even though its leaves hadn't come on yet, it was already covered with pinkish blooms. Ironic that something so lovely could now be a mortal enemy.

As she struggled to free herself, she heard someone crashing through the woods. Someone was following her! Fear gave her strength. With a loud ripping sound, she yanked the imprisoning material loose and dashed away, the torn patch of Gore-Tex flapping down against her pistoning legs.

She hurdled over fallen logs and limboed under low-hanging branches, but the sound of running footsteps behind her came ever closer. Her breath rattled in her throat. It was like a nightmare where you ran and ran from an unseen monster but could never get away. She had already done this once today. A terrible sense of *déjà vu* threatened to overcome her.

She strong-armed her way through a curtain of heavy hemlock boughs at breakneck speed, then without warning a cliff edge opened before her like a great yawning mouth. She skidded to a stop just in time to prevent herself from hurtling over the brink.

Hurriedly, she counted her options. The mountain fell away with a fairly smooth face for a good fifty feet then leveled out to a floor of rough and jagged rocks, before the heavy tree growth began again. Far away she could just make out the coastline and the ocean, but there wasn't a house or road in sight. There was no time to worry about that now; she had more immediate concerns.

She could see no way to get down safely. It was too far to jump and too steep and smooth to climb.

She struggled to control her breathing. It was roaring in her ears, but she tried to focus on listening intently. She thought she'd put some distance between herself and her pursuer. Perhaps she could angle back into the woods away from his direct path.

But then a sharp rattle of loosen stones startled her. It sounded as loud as a snare drum. Whoever had kicked the rocks couldn't be more than a few dozen feet away on the other side of the curtain of evergreen boughs.

April whirled first one way then the other in a terror of indecision. She felt as wobbly as a child's top running out of speed. Where should she run? Should she try to hide? What should she do?

The decision was taken away from her, as she suddenly lost her footing at the edge of the cliff. In horror she felt herself lose her balance and step off into space, her arms flailing as she went down.

She opened her mouth to scream, but only a dry gargle came out. She fleetingly thought that at least if she survived the fall she would have escaped from whoever had come after her. If he wasn't the one who had ended up with the gun, that is.

As she tumbled over the edge, her hands scrabbled frantically for purchase among a cluster of roots that grew out through the cliff face. She just managed to grasp one as she slid down. Her shoulders seem to leap out of their sockets as her arms took the impact of her full weight. A shower of dirt and rocks hit her square in her upturned face. But she had stopped her descent. She sobbed with relief and terror.

The sobs turned to hiccups, as she tried to control herself. She couldn't imagine being in a position any more ridiculous and dangerous, dangling between an enemy above and sharp rocks below.

She listened in an agony of suspense for what seemed an eternity. She heard nothing but the rasp of her breathing and the rattle and slide of small stones, as her weight on the roots eroded the dirt around them. How long would it be before the roots gave way and let her drop? She tried to hold her trembling body still. She didn't dare try to pull herself up and wasn't sure she could anyway even if she had the courage to attempt it.

Her arms and shoulders ached. Her hands felt raw against the slippery roots. Her eyes and mouth were full of dust and dirt. She blinked at the veil of grit.

Then she heard it. The swish of parting tree boughs and footsteps. They marched right up to the cliff edge above her and stopped. The sound boomed and echoed in her head. She waited, very near hysteria. Then finally, slowly, a hand appeared over the top of the cliff and reached down toward her.

Ten

"A nice day for just hanging out, eh kid?" Tyler said, his voice as close to jocular as the tension in his throat would allow.

A muffled squeak was the only reply.

Lying at full length, carefully testing the edge of the rock to make sure it wouldn't give way, he slowly eased his upper body far enough over the lip of the cliff to where he could see April. If the rim crumbled, he'd take her down with him.

When her upturned, frightened face came into his field of vision, he swallowed a bitter curse as he realized only a few puny roots were between her and a nasty fall to what would probably be her death or, at the very least, serious injury. He ground his teeth together against the terrible anger that shook him. She should never have been exposed to such danger and fear. He commanded his body to be still. He needed rock calm and steadiness now.

She had managed to hang onto the architectural plans. Mocking him, the damned tube that contained the blueprints that had lured her into this peril still protruded from the shoulder bag swinging from her back. He clenched his hands into fists, wanting in his frustration to rip the blueprints to shreds.

A ray of sun broke clear of the leaden sky and turned her hair into a blaze of fire around her pale, mud-and-blood-caked face. Dirt beaded her eyelashes and darkened her lips. Her clothes were ripped, and the bits of skin exposed were bruised, but she was the most beautiful sight he'd ever seen.

"Hang on, a few more inches and I'll be able to reach you," he said as reassuringly as he knew how in the face of the dozens of huge, jagged boulders leering up at him.

Apprehension showed plainly on her pixie face, more even than any sane person would feel with their very life dangling from a few threads of root. A good deal of that apprehension seemed to be directed at him. A dart of pain pierced his heart. She clearly didn't trust him.

Smith had planted little seeds of doubt. And his own behavior had provided a good climate for them to grow. How he wished he could go back to that magic moment in the forest when he held her in his arms, and she glowed with faith and an indefinable something more.

"Take my hand, April," he said gently, staring into her huge green eyes, willing her to believe in him again. "I can pull you up."

"I... I'm afraid to let go," she said, her teeth chattering.

"You can do it. Just pretend you're shaking hands. Reach out with your right hand. Hang on with your left. One hand at a time. That's all there is to it."

He tried to talk her through the steps they needed to take, but still he saw uncertainty troubling her face. Could she actually believe he'd fling her down the cliff?

He couldn't stop himself from thinking again of how trusting she'd been when they'd lain together among the whispering ferns. How she'd instinctively responded to his every lead. He'd give anything to have that trust back.

"April," he coaxed, "remember how easily I picked you up at the cabin. You're as light as a feather. It's a cinch. You can be up here and safe in just a few seconds."

He inched out a little further over the edge of the cliff. His hands weren't far from hers now. *If only she'd reach up!*

"Come on, ready now," he commanded. "One, two..."

He saw resolve take shape in her eyes. *God, she is brave!* Her body tensed in readiness. She had more courage and heart than any person he'd ever known.

She strained upward and clasped his hand. It felt no larger than a child's. He felt a roar of possession when he enveloped it in his own.

But during the moment that she reached for his hand, all her weight was suspended from just one root. The extra pull loosened a hailstorm of rocks and dirt that descended upon her unprotected face. Her body swayed dangerously. He lunged forward to grab her other hand, then struggled backward, pulling with all his might. April's feet scrabbled against the cliff wall, trying to gain purchase. She scrambled up beside him and collapsed in a heap on top of the cliff. She was safe!

But he'd leaned out too far trying to save her. The last tug on his hands as April released them to claw her way up and over the cliff rim had been his undoing. He twisted his upper body, clutching at the grasses that grew up to the cliff's edge, but it was too late. Head first, he slid over the top.

For a split second he was too stunned to react. Then self-preservation took over. His muscles automatically recalled the hours of drilling on his college diving team. He flipped in midair, righting himself. He'd land with his legs bent to absorb some of the force of the impact. He hoped.

Down, down, down he plummeted. He seemed to fall forever. Was this what his parents had experienced when they slipped down the face of the glacier? For the first time since their deaths, he felt a curious bond with them, as the rocks soared up to meet him.

Crash! The incredible impact jolted up his whole body. But wasn't there the tiniest bit of spring under his feet? Several decades of pine needles, maybe. He tucked and rolled, miraculously finding a path through the sharp rocks to absorb some of the tremendous energy generated by the momentum of his fall before his tumbling body finally exploded into a boulder and crumpled to rest.

He looked up and saw April's face far away floating above the cliff like an ethereal little cloud. She would run away from him now while she could, he thought hazily. But that was okay. At least she was safe. His last thought as sky, cliff, rocks and pain all drifted away was that, in spite of everything, he'd managed to save her.

~ * ~

April stared down in horror. "Tyler," she screamed over and over. But only a faint echo of her own voice bounced back to her. He didn't stir. "Please answer me," she whispered.

Please, please be all right, she begged silently as she trotted along the top of the cliff, searching for a way down. Finally, she came to a section of the cliff that sloped more gently to the forest floor. Outcroppings of large rocks looked as though they might provide hand and foot holds on the steeper parts. She was pretty sure she could make it without falling.

Throwing caution for her own safety aside, she skidded and slid down the mountainside, finishing with a stumbling run at the bottom where she was rushing so fast she only just barely managed to come to a stop without losing her footing.

Without pausing to get her breath, she hurried back along the bottom of the cliff, searching for Tyler. As she approached him, her heart froze. He lay so still! His legs and arms were twisted into odd shapes. His head was tucked awkwardly under one of his arms. Surely no living human could take such a strange form. It looked more as though some cruel practical jokester had thrown down a pile of tattered clothing.

Fearfully, she dropped down by his side. She wanted to throw herself on the rubble of dirt and pebbles and howl like an abandoned animal, but she knew she had to stay calm. Tyler's very life might depend on her self-control and resourcefulness. She prayed she could help him.

Should she try to untangle his head and limbs? In normal circumstances where an ambulance would be on its way to the scene of the accident, she knew you weren't supposed to move the victim. Tyler might have a spinal injury or concussion.

But no medics were coming here. April swallowed hard. She either had to move him or abandon him while she went for help. *If he can be helped.* The world seemed to spin around her at that thought. She narrowed her eyes and tensed her muscles, defying the dizziness. She refused to think that way. He would be all right.

She dropped her head and covered her eyes with one hand as she tried to determine the best course of action. But she knew she could never leave him behind as she searched for aid. And anyway, who knew how long it would take to find someone? It might be days. He could never survive alone and exposed like this. She was his only hope.

Determinedly, she shoved her hair back away from her face and rubbed dirt and grit from her eyes. She leaned forward and carefully eased his arm up and away from his neck.

He moaned incoherently. With a rush of relief, April let out the breath of air she hadn't realized she'd been holding.

"Oh, Tyler, thank God! You're alive!" she sobbed.

She yanked the shoulder bag strap from across her back and chest and pulled out the jug of water. She poured a little water through his slightly parted lips.

Sputtering and gasping, eyes blinking open, Tyler raised his head. He grinned crookedly. "You didn't run away."

"Of course I didn't run away," she said indignantly as she unconsciously continued to trickle water over his face.

He shook his head, drops of water flying. "April, I may have split my head open, but you really don't need to wash away what few brains I have left."

She jerked the jug away and capped it, flushing with embarrassment. "I'm sorry. I'm just so glad to see you're all right; I guess I don't know quite what I'm doing."

"Well," he groaned as he straightened his legs and rolled over on his back, "I wouldn't say I was exactly all right, but I'm glad you're pleased at the possibility. A little while ago I was pretty darn sure you were planning to shoot me."

April blushed more deeply. Her face burned with shame. She threw herself against his shirtfront and buried her face against his chest. "I'm so sorry," she wept. "Everything was so confusing. I didn't have time to think. And now you're lying here like this because you came back to help me. I'm so very sorry. Please forgive me."

April felt his chest rise against her cheek, as he took a long shuddering breath then let it out slowly. His arms encircled her. He crushed her against his body and threaded one hand through her hair. His voice was ragged.

"It's okay, April. I don't ever want to hurt you again. I acted like a selfish bastard, taking advantage of you in these weird circumstances when I knew all along it wasn't right—that we're too different—that I was just living for the moment. And Smith is one slick-talking con-artist. I don't blame you for doubting me."

She pulled away and dashed the tears from her eyes. "Tyler," she huffed, "here I was feeling more or less favorably inclined toward you and ashamed of myself for ever thinking you might be some kind of a crook, and you have to go and spoil it all with that 'we aren't right for each other' stuff. If you even think of saying one more time I'm the wrong woman, I might have to hit you."

He chuckled ruefully then rolled onto his side and tried to get up. She caught the grimace of pain cross his face. "What hurts? Is it your head?" she asked anxiously.

He carefully turned his head from side to side. "No. I'm a little groggy, but I don't think I actually hit my head on anything. It's my legs, especially along the shin here and this ankle," he said, pulling up his pants legs and pointing to the parts that pained him the most.

He gingerly tried to flex his ankle, and his face instantly contorted with pain. "It hurts like blazes," he said unnecessarily, "and it doesn't want to move when I tell it to."

"See if you can stand on it. I'll help you get up."

April's heart sank as he slowly rose to his feet. In spite of leaning heavily on her for support, he was unable to suppress a low moan. He was so big and so very heavy. What would they do, if he couldn't walk?

"I'll be your crutch," she said. "Let's see if we can at least get to the cover of the trees. If Smith or one of his gang should come this way, we'd be exposed here in this open place."

Tyler hobbled toward the sanctuary of evergreens, his mouth set in a grim line against the pain, a slick of perspiration forming on his forehead. At each step forward, when he put most of his weight on April, it was all she could do to stay on her feet.

The disparity in their heights made the going even more difficult. Tyler had to reach over so far to lean on April's shoulder it made it hard for him to keep his balance as he awkwardly shuffled and hopped.

Finally, they reached the concealing forest edge. Tyler eased down on a broad, flat rock. April sank down gratefully beside him. Both of them were panting.

"It's no good, April. We can't go on this way. You'll have to leave me here."

"I won't."

He wound one of her curls around his forefinger then gently blew it away. Tenderly, he ran a finger over the curve of her cheek.

Enough dirt encrusted her face that he could probably finger paint, she thought.

"You're a trooper," he said admiringly, "and I'm grateful, but I can't walk anymore. Surely you can see that."

"Then we'll just have to find another way," she replied stubbornly. "I'll think of something."

"If just one leg were injured, we could probably fashion makeshift crutches out of tree branches, but neither leg can bear any weight. I think there's some kind of fracture along my shin, and my ankle is either badly sprained or broken, too."

He grasped her upper arm with one strong hand and clasped her chin with the other, forcing her to look at him. "Listen to me. Help me get comfortable here. Leave me the water and those cattails you gathered. We can make a kind of bed with leaves and pine needles and a cover with my raincoat. Then go. It'll be dusk soon. Without me to slow you down, you might still be able to find someone before dark."

April's eyes lit up. Impatiently, she shook herself free from his grasp and jumped up off the rock. "Your raincoat! That's it! I'll make a travois."

"A what?"

Already busily searching the downed timber for the right shape and length of branches, she barely heard him. "A travois. You know, like the Native Americans used. I'll fasten your raincoat to a couple of branches, and I can pull you."

"There's no way I'm going to let you pull me over this rough terrain, and you wouldn't be able to do it anyway, even if I'd let you, which I won't."

Seeking to reassure him, April paused long enough in her search to push up her jacket and jersey sleeves to flex her biceps. "See, I'm lots stronger than I look."

For a moment he stared at her exposed arm with the kind of expression in his eyes that reminded her of the way he had stroked her arms and legs and every other imaginable part of her body only a few hours ago. Her breath caught in her throat with an audible little click.

But then the tiny lines around his eyes crinkled, and the corners of his mouth twitched suspiciously. He wasn't thinking about making love to her at all; he was laughing at her! She yanked her sleeve down. He must think she looked like a little kid bragging about her muscles.

"I know you're strong, April," he said. "That's not the point."

She turned her back on him to hide the flush of anger and embarrassment suffusing her face over his amusement and resumed her search. "If you're worried about the bumpy ride jostling you around, don't. I'll rig up the raincoat so well, you'll think you're resting in a hammock."

She turned to face him. "And anyway, whether you like it or not, you can't very well run away from me, can you? You might as well lie back and enjoy the trip, because one way or another, you are going to be carried out of here."

He clenched his jaw and crossed his arms over his chest. "Over my dead body."

"That, too, could be arranged," she said as she menaced him with a short, knobby branch of cedar.

He reached up to grasp the thick stick and, with one quick, powerful yank, pulled her down beside him and into his arms. He silenced her startled shriek with his soft, warm mouth.

"April," he muttered against her traitorous, all-too-willing lips, "you're the most exasperating woman I've ever met. Whatever am I going to do with you?"

She longed to stay right where she was because, after this morning's incredible joining, she now knew exactly what he could do with her, but time was passing far too quickly. She sighed, savoring the last hot thrust of his tongue, then squirmed out of his arms. She could barely breath.

"Getting late." She struggled to speak rationally. "Got to find those branches."

She widened her search until she found some tree limbs that, with some trimming, she thought would do. And then she found something else even more important. Dragging the two long branches behind her, she ran back to where Tyler sat.

"Tyler, Tyler! I've found some kind of trail. It's an abandoned logging road, I think. It's a little overgrown, but it'll be so much easier to pull you on it than through the forest around all the bushes and stumps and things. I think we can actually make it."

She paused, realizing she'd just revealed a lack of confidence she'd been trying to keep strictly to herself. "Not that we couldn't have made it through the forest, too, of course," she finished a shade defensively.

He grinned at her. "Of course."

A trifle uncertain, she echoed his grin.

"Here," he said, reaching out toward her, "hand me one of those branches. I'll clean it for you."

With a rush of glad relief and a genuine smile stretching her lips wide, she gave him the branch. *Thank goodness.* He was going to help. They were partners again. In her heart she had known all along that without his cooperation she never would have been able to get him away from here.

They both began to pull away the smaller twigs and strip away the bark from the tree limbs until they had two fairly smooth, long poles of approximately the same size. April took the branch Tyler had been working on and held it upright in front of her along with her own. She squinted along their length from top to bottom.

"Not bad," she said, "I think they'll do. Now for the raincoat."

She pulled it out of her shoulder bag. "I need something to cut with. What a shame I stopped carrying my Swiss Army knife in my pack."

"Some of the little rocks have pretty sharp edges." Tyler poked his finger through one of the myriad rips and holes that pocked his trousers and suit coat. "I can attest to that."

April combed the undergrowth until she found a rock that suited her needs. "Now for your tie. I hope you didn't throw it away."

Tyler chuckled as he pulled the burgundy and navy patterned tie out of his jacket pocket and handed it over to April. "So, they really are good for something besides the corporate image. I always wondered."

Sawing vigorously at the fine silk fabric, April cut the tie into short lengths then proceeded to thread the strips through the buttonholes of the raincoat to fasten it along the end of one of the poles. Next, she hacked at the opposite edge of the raincoat to cut slits so she could tie that side to the other pole.

"Whew," she said, as she wiped away the sweat threatening to run into her eyes, "this raincoat is a lot harder to get through than the tie."

"Rest for awhile. Give me the rock. I can do that."

April took advantage of Tyler's bent head, as he labored on the raincoat, to observe him without his being aware of her close scrutiny. His clothing and body had taken a terrible beating, but she'd never before met a man to whom she felt so attracted. He looked like a ragbag, and it didn't make a whit of difference. She wanted him with an intensity that frightened her.

It was a miracle he was alive. He'd survived a killer fall with relatively minor injuries. *Unless, at this very minute, some vital internal organ is allowing his lifeblood to leak away.*

A freezing wave of fear threatened to overwhelm her, endangering her very breathing. She struggled to draw in a sustaining gulp of the rapidly cooling, cedar-scented air. Night would be upon them soon.

She simply had to get him out of here—to medical attention and back to his safe world where men fought their battles with silk ties, not with revolvers. No matter that she'd never see him again once he returned to his own territory.

Pain crushed her to the forest floor. She lay back and squeezed her eyes shut against the agony. It was unendurable. She wasn't sure she could live without the man she loved.

April shot upright like a released spring. *Love! It couldn't be.* How could she think such a thing? She'd only known him for one day. And Tyler was right; they really were all wrong for each other. They came from different worlds, had different interests and values.

Tyler wanted an old-fashioned, traditional family with a wife who catered to her husband and children. *Could I be that woman?* She honestly didn't know. She loved children and found the exploits of her many nieces and nephews endlessly fascinating, but could her family ever be her whole life? There were so many places she hadn't seen yet, so many things she hadn't done. Could she give up her dreams to become a wife and mother?

He raised his head and smiled at her when she sat up. His smile was warm and full of humor, and his beautiful dark eyes made her feel all liquid and melting inside. She tried to smile back at him but could only manage a crooked grimace. Fortunately, he didn't seem to notice as he bent his head again to his work.

"You weren't kidding," he said. "This material is really tough. It's a struggle, but I'm almost finished. One more hole, and it'll be ready to go."

She stared at him, imprinting memories of his every beloved feature into her brain. She would never forget him, because as impossible and strange as it might seem, she knew in her heart that what she felt for this man was love.

Perhaps it really was only because of the intensity of the experiences they had shared over the past few excruciating hours, but somehow, for her, the attraction of two opposites had been melded into one overpowering love.

She sighed deeply and rose to her feet. Not that they could ever make a go of it, anyway, for even if Tyler loved her back, which he clearly didn't and wouldn't, there remained the sticking point that neither of them could ever fit into the other's life. If she questioned the image of her molding herself into his vision of what a man and woman should be to one another and to their children, it was even more impossible to imagine him joining her in a quest to see the world.

She would just have to find a way to get over the hurt no matter what the cost.

With great force Tyler rubbed the sharp stone one last time over the stubborn raincoat material, and it gave way with a ripping sound that seemed to April to come from her very heart.

"Yes!" Tyler said, throwing up his arms like a sprinter who's just won a race. "That should do it."

Struggling to hide her painful thoughts, April took the raincoat and tied it to the bottom of the remaining tree limb. Then she crossed the poles at their thicker end, forming a long, asymmetrical "x", and lashed them together with the raincoat's belt at the point where they crossed.

Out of the corner of her eye, she saw Tyler studying her as she worked.

"There," she said with false brightness, "it's ready. Let's give it a try."

"April, come here," Tyler said quietly.

She approached him reluctantly. He gently pulled her down beside him on the flat rock, his eyes searching hers as he questioned her. "There's something wrong, isn't there? If you've changed your mind about this travois thing, it's okay to say so."

He grinned at her in the charmingly boyish, light-hearted way she loved so much. "You might have noticed I didn't think much of the plan from the start, so it's fine with me if you want to give it up."

He wiped away a tear that, in spite of her best efforts at control, had managed to escape down her cheek.

"We'll revert to Plan A, and I'll stay here, while you look for help. Or, if you've come up with Plan C, we'll go with that."

He kissed her on the nose then captured another disobedient tear. "Whatever it takes, April, to put a glow back on your face. I can't stand seeing you like this. What happened to the wild, impetuous April who can do anything with one arm tied behind her back? The mad woman I've come to know and love."

Eyes wide, April stared at him. *Love?* But of course, he was only teasing. It was just an expression. He had no idea how important the word was to her or what she had been thinking about.

"It's not the travois, Tyler," she said miserably. "I still think I can pull you out of here. It's... Oh, I don't know. Just that everything is so overwhelming right now."

He pulled her into a reassuring bear hug against his hard, warm body. "It's certainly that, April. It's certainly that."

April sighed and melted into the comfort of his arms. If only she could stay right where she was forever.

Eleven

Tyler gave her one last hard squeeze then pulled back far enough to look at her. "Better?" he questioned as he examined her face.

She nodded, swiped at the remaining pesky tears and tried not to snuffle.

"So, what's it to be?" he asked. "The final decision. Plan A, B or C?"

She smiled shakily. "The travois. At least let's see if it'll work."

"Bring it over next to me, and I'll try it on for size."

April positioned the makeshift travois beside Tyler, and he eased his long frame onto the raincoat. Taking a deep breath, she took her place at the other end of the travois and lifted the poles. The raincoat sagged under Tyler's weight, but his body cleared the ground.

"Wagons, ho!" Tyler sang out.

"Not funny," April grumbled, giving him a dirty look back over her shoulder.

Fitting the poles snugly under her armpits, she strained forward, pulling with all her might. Nothing happened. She groaned inwardly. *Oh, no! It just has to work.* She didn't have a Plan C.

"Broken axle already?"

April turned her head to glare at him. "Didn't anyone ever tell you nobody likes a wise guy?"

He grinned broadly at her as he lay back comfortably with his hands laced behind his head, looking for all the world like a man relaxing in a chaise lounge while on vacation. All he needed to complete the picture was a tall frosty glass with a paper umbrella and a slice of lime perched on the rim.

She faced forward again and took several deep breaths, firming her resolve and focusing her energy on the task. "The Native Americans used dogs to pull these things. If a mutt could do it, so can I."

She let up on the pressure she was exerting and backed up a half step then lunged forward as hard as she could. The ends of the travois lurched an inch or two over the bumpy ground.

"Yahoo!" Tyler whooped. "Atta girl. Now we're rolling. Keep it up."

"It seems," April huffed, "to work better," she puffed, "if I don't stop. Momentum," she gasped, "makes it easier," she wheezed, "to pull."

After what seemed an eternity of backbreaking labor, she reached the old logging trail. She threw down the poles, depositing Tyler none too gently on the ground, and collapsed on her back next to him, breathing hard.

Tyler rose up on his elbows and peered at her. "You're doing great, April. I never thought you could pull me."

"It would help if you weren't so darned big," April groaned as she used the back of her hand to wipe sweat from her forehead. "If I had to get stranded in a wilderness with somebody, I don't see why he couldn't have been a ninety pound weakling."

"I'm rapidly turning into one. With both legs out of commission, I'd say that was pretty weak. I really hate it that you have to drag me out of here." He banged his clinched fist against his thigh. "It's so unfair."

"Fair, shmair. You wouldn't need to be dragged if you hadn't saved me from the cliff. If I couldn't walk, you'd do the same for me. Though," she finished with a twinkle in her eye, "I really don't weigh much more than ninety pounds."

"I'll probably catch up with you before we get out of here. I'm shrinking fast. I'll bet I've lost at least twenty pounds already." He rubbed his flat stomach ruefully. "Hear that rumble? Why don't you break out the cattails? You'll need the energy if you're going to make it the rest of the way."

April divided the last of the cattails and berries evenly between them, ignoring Tyler's protests that she needed most of the food since she was doing all of the work. They munched together companionably. Even the bitter berries tasted pretty good by now, but there wasn't nearly enough. Hunger gnawed at her so intensely it was almost like pain.

Then she remembered something else the ecology teacher had said at Camp Waskowitz when she was twelve. She grabbed the sharp cutting stone she had carried along with them, leaped up, ran over to one of the smaller hemlocks and began hacking away at the bark.

"What the... ! April, what the Sam Hill or you doing now?" Tyler called after her.

"Getting us some more food."

Tyler groaned. "You're not looking for ants or worms, are you? Because I absolutely draw the line at eating insects or slimy things."

"If you got hungry enough, a bug would probably look like a delicacy, but that's not what I'm trying to find now."

She pulled away a large section of the outer bark then cut at the green growing layer just underneath it. She carried big pieces of the cambium back to where Tyler lay waiting and handed one of them to him.

"Here, try this."

He sniffed at it gingerly. "Smells a little like pasta. Looks a little like it, too."

He took a bite. "Why, it's good! Chewy and kind of sweet."

April ate some, too. She was shocked. It really was good. "You needn't sound so surprised."

She didn't say just how very surprised she was herself. "You ought to recognize my culinary talents by now."

"Oh, believe me, April, I do recognize your many talents," Tyler said in a husky voice, staring at her with an intensity that was disconcerting.

April looked away, flushing warmly. Beauty surrounded them. Long lances of dusk's golden light pierced the majestic evergreens to illuminate a sprawling exotica of lovely, strange ferns and mosses growing thickly over the forest floor. Dozens of varieties of plants she'd never seen before thrived here. They had stumbled into a fairyland.

A frog peeped tentatively, then was joined by another. Soon hundreds of croaking voices joined to sing a lusty mating chorus of frogsong.

It was a magical place. What fun it would be to come back properly outfitted.

She turned back to Tyler to say so and was confronted by his intense, dark eyes still watching her.

She shivered. But of course it could never be. Tyler only wanted to get away from the wilderness and her, never to return. Her excitement over the beauty of this wild, remote place would only remind him of his parents and his pain.

"April," Tyler whispered, "you have the most remarkable eyes. They always seem to be dancing."

He gathered her to him and kissed her deeply. Instantly, her body was alive with desire for him. It throbbed deep within her.

He moved slightly away and moaned. "How can it be? Starving to death with two broken legs, probably in shock, and all I can think of is making love to you. You're some kind of witch. You've cast a spell on me."

She slipped out of his grasp and spoke lightly, trying to hide the heaviness of her heart. "It's just the trauma. It knocks your emotions all out of whack. You won't remember any of this when you get home."

She turned away from him so she wouldn't have to see the expression on his face when she mentioned home, then she anxiously looked at their surroundings more closely. "It's getting dark. We've got to get going."

She resumed her position at the head of the travois and started down the logging path. The going was a little easier on the smoother terrain, though she occasionally had to push aside some brush. A downhill slope helped to a certain extent, but it still took a huge effort to move Tyler along.

"It's really a shame we had to leave my bike behind. I'll bet I could have rigged up some kind of cart with the wheels. That would have been a lot easier to pull."

"I have absolutely no doubt you could have made the queen's coach if you'd wanted to. I think you can probably do anything you set your mind to—if it doesn't get too boring."

April flinched. He was damning her with his extravagant praise.

"I can stick to something, if it's worthwhile, even if it does get a little tedious sometimes," she protested.

"What about a husband and family? Would you consider that worthwhile?"

She wanted to shout "yes" with all her heart, if Tyler was the husband, but she wasn't sure she honestly could. Her mother handled the job beautifully, seemingly having fun in the bargain, and so did her sisters and her aunts, but could she?

She bent even harder to the task at hand, lurching miserably down the mountainside in silence, not answering his question, the travois jolting along behind her.

It was getting dark far too quickly; she could only see a few feet in front of her. The road was fairly narrow, having been made originally just wide enough to accommodate a single logging truck. The tall trees on either side of the trail blocked most of the waning light.

"We're going to have to stop pretty soon. I can't see where I'm going."

"Another night alone together in the woods," Tyler said gloomily.

Stung, April pulled harder. He clearly couldn't stand the idea of spending a moment longer with her than was absolutely necessary. Gritting her teeth, she strained against the strength-sapping load. She'd haul him out of the forest tonight, if it killed her.

Anxiously, she strained her eyes trying to see what lay in front of them. How much farther could it be to the coast? She'd seen the ocean from the top of the cliff. Surely, they were getting close by now.

Was it her overactive imagination, or was there a shade more light up ahead? There was! She was sure of it. It must mean there was a break in the trees only a little distance away.

She decided not to say anything to Tyler. She didn't want to get his hopes up if she was wrong, but she made a superhuman effort to pick up the pace. The travois bounced along behind her, until suddenly, they emerged from the shadowy trees into the relatively brighter light of a glorious coastal sunset.

April dropped the poles and danced through the sand and pebbles toward the lapping ocean. The sun was a giant ball of fire just dipping into the sea. Reflected crimson, orange and gold streaked the water. Several heavily wooded, tiny islands hugged the curving shoreline.

"Tyler, we made it! We really made it."

Tyler was sitting up on the raincoat, looking around with maddeningly stodgy calm. He didn't seem in the least impressed with her Herculean effort.

"But made it to where?" he queried. "I don't see any houses or a road. It's just as desolate here as it was in the forest. We still have a long way to go."

Deflated as a popped birthday balloon, April sank down on the beach. Tyler sure knew how to take the fun out of things, but of course, he was absolutely right. She looked up and down the beach. Nothing. Nothing but the most absolutely fantastically gorgeous coastline and sunset she'd ever seen.

"I guess we'd better try to set up some kind of camp here, then," she said, all the energy gone from her voice. The brilliant colors in the sky dulled as she spoke. "I don't think I can go any farther today."

"April... " Tyler said in a low voice that held a terrible warning.

April's head snapped up. Surely, it was only a horrible illusion brought on by fatigue or a nightmare mirage caused by the fading sunset.

But no, it was real. Three men emerged from the trees quite a way down the coast. They didn't all come out on the beach at the same spot but were spaced many yards apart. Each of the three carried a short, blunt, metallic object in his hand, unmistakable even at a distance in the fitful light.

At the sight her scalp prickled, and a disturbing sensation slithered down the back of her neck.

"Must have fanned out, searching for us," Tyler said. "I wonder what happened to Stolz. Do you think Smith sent these guys looking for us before or after our encounter with him?"

"Who cares!" She could hear the hysteria edging her voice. "They're here now."

His jaw tightened, but his voice was still gallingly calm. "It might make a difference eventually. If Stolz got away, he'll send help."

She could feel her muscles bunching as she half rose into a crouch. "But we've got to escape now. There isn't any help in sight, and I can't pull you fast enough to run away. They'd catch us in just a few minutes. Do you think we can hide in the woods?"

He looked at the trees. "No. We're down low, the light's bad, but as soon as we start moving, they'll see us if they haven't already. You're right. We couldn't make it very far. We're too slow. Even in the dark, they'd find us sooner or later."

Frantically, April tried to think. The men were now clearly confident of their prize. They had caught up with one another and now walked three abreast along the beach. They moved slowly, but inexorably through the gloom straight for Tyler and her.

"There's only one way for us to go," Tyler said. He sounded strangely resigned. "We'll have to swim for it."

April's mouth dropped open. She looked with fear and dread at the ocean she'd thought so beautiful only a few minutes before.

The surf was fairly calm, but she knew the water was desperately cold. There was a little island not too terribly far from the shore. She thought she might be able to swim that length in warm water if she weren't already exhausted. But the Pacific Northwest coast was so far north that the sea was bone-numbingly frigid all year round, and their bodies had already taken so much punishment over the past day and a half. She was pretty sure they were on one of the San Juan Islands. She was absolutely sure they could only survive a few minutes in the freezing Straits of San Juan De Fuca.

"Tyler, no. I can't... " she whispered.

Her voice trailed off, for he was already on his hands and knees, crawling toward the water, one leg dragging behind him in the sand.

Reluctantly, April followed, staying low to the ground, too, so less of her body would be exposed to the three men. She noted Tyler wasn't crawling straight toward the water but was snaking back and forth in an indirect path, taking advantage of the cover offered by huge, sun-bleached and pebble-polished logs that had washed up on the beach. She soon caught up and stayed close behind him.

Tyler paused when they were only a few feet from the water. They were well concealed from the men by a gigantic tree that had made it to the shore with its twisted, gnarled roots intact. April shuddered. It resembled a giant Medusa head silhouetted against the darkening sky. The incoming waves washed the tip of the tree, alternately lifting it high then dropping it back to the sand. Thousands of pebbles made a rattling sound as the spent waves receded.

"Hurry," Tyler said as he pulled off his shoes and suit coat. "Get rid of anything that might pull you down. I don't think they can tell exactly where we are right now. Hopefully, they'll think we're just trying to hide and won't realize we're going to swim."

He flinched as a sudden thought seemed to strike him. "You can swim, can't you?"

"Of course I can swim! But do you know how cold that water is? And you're injured. I don't think we can make it."

"I don't see that at this point we have much choice. The cold will deaden the pain in my legs, and anyway, I can swim with just my arms if I have to."

His stern expression rebuked her. "Please don't waste time arguing, April. We need every second to get as far out in the water as we can before they see us. If we're really quiet and very lucky, they might not even notice us in the water."

April took off her radio holster and her fanny pack. She ripped off her arm pouch and her shoes. "I'm ready," she said.

"The shoulder bag," he said, tugging at it. "It'll fill with water and pull you down like a stone."

She shrugged away from him. "Maybe not. It's waterproof. I think it'll float if the top stays up high enough. I've brought it this far. I don't want to throw the evidence away now."

He let go of the strap. "Can you get out of it, if it's in your way?"
She nodded.

"Promise?" he whispered harshly.

She nodded again, her jaw clenched, trying to keep her teeth from chattering with fear.

He pressed a brief hard kiss against her rigid lips then slid into the waves without another sound. As he entered the water, the rim of the sun sizzled behind the ocean's horizon, taking with it the last of the evening's light and leaving behind a dark and forbidding sea.

April crawled into the brine. The first shock of cold against her arms and chest was so extreme, for a second she couldn't think or move or breath. Then, as her overwhelmed nervous system screamed to life, it took every ounce of self-control not to shriek or flail against the enveloping frigid grip. She spit salty water out of her mouth, as icy waves slapped her in the face.

The shore fell away sharply. In only a few moments she could no longer touch bottom. Tyler was just ahead, treading water, waiting for her.

He smiled encouragingly at her, apparently not willing to risk even a whisper, then grinned in amusement as he pointed at her shoulder bag. She could feel it bobbing out behind her head. The empty plastic milk jug inside must be acting like a buoy, she thought, floating and thereby holding the whole bag up high in the water. She hoped it would work like a life preserver and hold her up, too, because the cold was sapping her strength at an alarmingly rate.

At first, reacting against the cold, she had been swimming quite fast, Tyler easily matching her stroke for stroke, but now she was slowing down. He looked very much at home in the water; he must be a regular swimmer. That might explain why, even though he was only a businessman, he seemed so fit.

But she wasn't doing so well. She couldn't feel her hands or feet; she wasn't even sure where they were in the water. She thought she was still kicking her legs, but she wasn't absolutely certain. The only reason she knew for sure her arms were still slowly windmilling around her head was that she could see them each time she dragged her face up out of the water for a gulp of air.

Her upper body felt slightly warmer. Maybe her close-fitting jacket was acting like a wetsuit, trapping an insulating layer of water warmed by body heat. She was glad she hadn't taken it off, glad Tyler hadn't insisted.

Dogpaddling for a moment, April raised her head high to get her bearings. They had put a pretty good distance between themselves and the coast. They were a little less than halfway to the island. But could she make it? Somehow, it looked even farther away now than it had when they were crouching on the shore.

Tyler paused when she did. He paddled next to her, an assessing expression on his face. Clearly, he was keeping close tabs on her progress. She was trying her hardest to smile at him when she heard the noise. There were shouts, then hollow popping sounds came from the beach, followed closely by a hail of plops in the water all around them.

Her body jerked spasmodically. The shock was even worse than when she hit the icy water. This time she couldn't help but scream. It didn't matter anyway, she thought in dismay, there was no longer any need for silence; they'd been discovered.

"Come on," Tyler yelled, powering through the water with strong, sure strokes.

April tried to emulate him, but her arms and legs were too numb to respond to her frantic request for more speed. Even her lungs refused to work properly; all of her chest and diaphragm muscles were slowing down from the cold. She couldn't get enough air.

Gasping for breath, she miscalculated the position of her head in the water and sucked in a lungful of the salty brine. Coughing and choking, her lungs and nose burning, she moved erratically in the water. Then she went under the surface. Her eyes were wide open, as the dark waves closed over her head.

Terror gave her a spurt of energy. She flailed at the water, now her enemy, but only managed to raise her head above the surface for a moment. Not even long enough for a gulp of life-sustaining air. She went back down. There was a ringing in her head; she couldn't think clearly. Maybe she should just breathe in the alien substance and go peacefully.

As she sank, stars of light began to appear around her. Very pretty, she thought absently, trying to catch one in her hand. But her arms and legs didn't work at all now. They floated lazily, aimlessly around her body. The only sensation left was the powerful, all-consuming urge to breathe.

As the stars disappeared one by one and a great heavy darkness descended, she suddenly felt strong arms encircle her. They carried her up, up until her head popped above the water. The cold air stung at her face, as a river of water poured out of her mouth and nose.

"No," she sputtered and gurgled, "it was warmer down there."

Tyler's voice was grim in her ear, as his powerful arms towed her through the water. "You're confused, April. Hypothermia. Lack of oxygen. I've got you now. Relax."

He slid the strap of her now heavy shoulder bag off her shoulder. It must have filled with water when she'd pulled it under with her. Through a haze in front of her vision, she saw it sink into the sea. She tried to think. Something precious in there. Remembering, her kitten-weak arms struggled against him. "The blueprints! Got to save them. They're important."

"Not as important as you," he said fiercely. "Let them go."

April relaxed in his arms and tried to float to lighten his load. Even with the burden of her weight and his injuries, they moved rapidly through the water. What incredible strength and endurance!

Tears slowly leaked down her cheeks, burning hot against her cold skin. Only yesterday Tyler had risked his own life to secure the blueprints in the woods. Now he was willing to throw them away to save hers.

She looked back at the shore. She could just barely make out the three men in the remaining dim light. They appeared quite small, doll figures gesturing on the beach. Bullets still splated into the ocean, but she and Tyler were now several yards beyond the little splashes that rose where the ammo hit.

She tried to tell him. "W-W-We're out of r-range, I-I think." Her teeth clattered together so hard, she wasn't sure he could understand what she said.

"Good," he grunted. "The island's not too much farther. Try to kick your legs. It'll help you generate some body heat, and we might go a little faster."

She fluttered her legs. To coordinate that small movement took a supreme effort of will. Her muscles cramped and contracted at random, totally out of her control. Her body ached all over at a bone-deep level. She shook spasmodically.

She had begun to drift again into a hazy darkness, when Tyler's voice pulled her back. "Come on, April. Don't give up on me now. You can make it."

Struggling to help him push them through the water, she heard a new sound that stirred her to alertness. Waves! Waves stronger than the diminutive silvery whitecaps dancing around them. Waves slapping against a shore.

She kicked in earnest now with her last remaining sliver of strength. "Let me go, Tyler. I think I can make it in on my own. It'll be easier for you."

"No way. I got you this far. I'm not going to lose you now."

Together, they kicked and splashed and rode the waves until the surf deposited them upon a little patch of beach. They were lucky to have hit the sandy spot, April thought, because most of the island appeared to meet the ocean with a cliff. Trees grew almost down to the sea.

Tyler attempted to drag himself farther up on the pebbles and sand out of reach of the foam that was rolling his legs about like strands of limp spaghetti, but his arms gave out and he collapsed, still lying half in the ebb and flow of the water. April tried to crawl over to help him, but she couldn't move. Both of their bodies shivered and quaked uncontrollably.

April squeezed her eyes shut against the agony of cold. Wasn't freezing to death supposed to be painless? Weren't you just supposed to drift off into a peaceful sleep? But this hurt; it hurt terribly, even worse than when she'd burned her arm in boiling water, helping her mother can peaches.

With great effort, she forced her eyes open. Tyler still lay where his strength had given out, his face in the sand, his arms stretched out in front of him from trying to claw his way up the beach, his powerful biceps visibly quivering even through his torn, wet shirt.

He called her name, his voice terrifyingly faint. "April... "

Desperately, she tried to force out a response but couldn't manage one syllable. Even her vocal cords seemed to be frozen.

She looked up at the sky, the stars blurred by tears. A lovely pale, full moon stared back down at her. No help there. She squelched a bitter laugh at the absurdity and anguish of it all. What irony to have shared so many adventures and to have escaped from a dozen disasters only for Tyler and her to die together of exposure under the watchful eye of a cold and heartless moon.

Twelve

Tyler turned his head to the side and spat salt water out of his mouth, sand grating across his teeth. He tried to raise himself up on his forearms but fell back onto the beach. He gritted his teeth together, ignoring the grinding sand, and tried to get up again. He'd never let anything defeat him in the past, not even the death of his parents; he sure as hell wasn't going to let the ocean beat him now.

All at once he realized he didn't hear April's excited voice exclaiming over their swim. She had rejoiced enthusiastically over all of their previous escapes, where was she now? He struggled up to his hands and knees, looking for her. He desperately wanted to hear her bubbly voice, the voice that sounded as thrilled and delighted as a child after a roller coaster ride.

Then he saw her lying on her back not far from him, her pale face washed by moonlight. She looked very small and frighteningly silent.

He crawled over to her, though his legs and arms trembled so violently they could barely support his weight. He never remembered feeling so feeble. He sat beside her and gathered her limp body into his lap. Her head fell back. He kissed her forehead, her cheeks, her neck. Her skin was so cold! But his lips found a tiny pulse beating at her throat.

He had given up prayer after years of fervent requests for his parents to come back had gone unanswered, but he prayed silently now. *Please let her live,* he begged.

Her eyelids flickered then popped wide open. She seemed to recognize who held her and gave a gentle sigh of relief and acceptance. Tyler had never felt so needed. He pulled her tightly to him, pressing their icy cold cheeks together.

"About time you woke up," he said, his voice embarrassingly thick and choked. "I don't tolerate any sleeping on the job."

He thought she'd spring away with a tart retort, but she only sighed again and snuggled closer against his chest. Her whole body vibrated like a plucked bowstring. The shivering and her lack of response to his jibe alarmed him.

He shook her gently. "We can't stay here, April. We have to find some kind of shelter. We've got to get out of these wet clothes and get warm."

Craning his neck to check out their surroundings, he tried not to think about what the outcome would be if they didn't.

The little island that had become their refuge was heavily wooded. Trees grew close by the water. Perhaps if they took off their wet things and covered themselves with dry leaves and branches, they could generate enough body heat to survive the night. It wasn't much of a plan, but it was the only idea he could come up with at the moment.

He thought of the thick, fluffy goose down comforter on his bed at home. He'd give anything to be able to wrap it around April in front of a roaring blaze in his fireplace, maybe after a long soak in the hot tub.

Impatient with his wistful fantasy, he shook his head roughly. This wasn't the time for daydreams; they needed action, immediate action before they fell into hypothermic unconsciousness never to wake up again. The very fact that he was just sitting here instead of doing something was one of the signs of hypothermia—a lack of good judgment.

He ground out a curse, as a soft patter of rain suddenly formed tiny craters in the sand around them and turned dull pebbles shiny. So much for getting under dry leaves.

~ * ~

"What is it?" April mumbled.

"Rain. Can you move? We need to find shelter."

She stirred in his arms. "Maybe we can find another cave, like you did last night." She sat up and looked around, already searching for a place to go in spite of her weakness.

He smiled at the enthusiasm he heard building in her voice. *That's more like it.* No matter how down and out they might seem, he could count on April rising to the occasion. She loved a challenge. She might not be a woman he'd be willing to trust with his heart for the long haul of day-to-day life, but he'd never met anyone—man or woman—he'd rather be with in a life-or-death crisis.

Plucking at his sleeve to gain his attention, April pointed to the crest of the island above the little beach. "Look at the glint there. It's glass, isn't it? Moonlight reflecting off glass?"

Tyler stared in the direction she was pointing, hoping it wasn't an illusion. "Yes! You're right! And a roofline. The angle's too straight to be a tree branch. It's some kind of building. Let's go."

April staggered to her feet. Her legs wobbled like a newborn fawn's. "I'll run on ahead to see what's there. Maybe there's someone who can carry you."

Tyler snorted with laughter. "Braggart. What makes you think you can run? No, I'm coming, too. I need to keep moving."

He knew, in her weakened condition, April couldn't support his weight even for a short distance, so Tyler stayed on his hands and knees and crawled up the beach, not even attempting to walk. The way seemed long and hard, even though the beach was tiny.

"Ow!" April cried, hopping feebly on one bare foot while rubbing the other. "As frozen as my feet are, you wouldn't think stepping on these darn rocks would hurt so much."

"It's a good sign," Tyler grunted. He was waging the same battle against the rocks with his knees. Each time he dragged one of his legs forward, he felt a warm, wet seepage of blood. "Getting some feeling back means your circulation is improving."

Finally, they reached the woods. The going was even harder there, though the trees offered a little protection from the cold rain. Clouds obscured the moon; visibility was very poor. Tyler fought his way around and through the thick underbrush.

"Can't say much for this worm's eye view," he grumbled, as his hand slipped on a jumble of pinecones, and a clump of salal scratched his face.

April pushed on ahead of him, her easy grace gone. She awkwardly dragged herself across logs she would have easily leaped over earlier in the day. It hurt him to see the loss of her strength and beauty of movement.

She stumbled around a grove of spreading junipers and cried out. "It's real! I didn't imagine it. There really is a house. Hurry, Tyler!"

She waited for him, as he struggled to catch up with her, and they approached the house together. The forest grew almost up to the back door. There were no lights that he could see, though the veils of rain and his low position on the ground hindered his view.

"Someone's vacation house, I'd guess," he said.

The thrill of their discovery seemed to revive April's energy. She almost danced up to the door and knocked loudly. There was no answer. April pounded on the door. "Hello. Is there anyone there? We need help. Please open the door," she shouted. But there was no response.

"I'll try the front," she said and darted away.

Soon, Tyler heard a renewed thumping reverberate from the front of the house. It continued for a long time before the banging finally died away.

April reappeared, looking utterly forlorn, her shoulders sagging and rain dripping down her face. "There's no one here," she said.

Tyler picked up a large rock and hefted it. "Help me stand up," he commanded.

With April's assistance, he managed to pull himself to his feet. He ignored the excruciating stabs of pain and hobbled toward the door.

Oh, no," April gasped as she belatedly realized his purpose. "That's breaking and entering."

Tyler grinned as the rock crashed through the pane of glass. It was clear the cold had slowed down her usual quick thinking. "They'll forgive us, April. This is a desperate situation, an emergency. I'll pay for the damage."

Carefully, he reached around the remaining shards of glass, fumbled until he found the lock and opened the door. "Anyway, it'd be better to do the jail time than to die from the cold."

April worriedly gnawed at her lower lip then burst out, "But what if someone's in there, and they're just not answering the door?"

In the small amount of available light, he could see that her eyes were wide with apprehension.

"They might think we're burglars, or worse. If they keep a gun, they might shoot us."

"Come here, April."

Looking nervous, she gingerly stepped over broken pieces of glass lying on the stoop and the floor and entered the house. He leaned against the wall to support himself, pulled her into his arms, tilted her chin up and smoothed dripping locks of hair away from her face. She was still shivering uncontrollably. "You have a vivid imagination, did you know that?" She gave him a slightly embarrassed grin. Lightly, he kissed the curve of her mouth. "Whatever's in here, we'll deal with it. Okay?

She nodded and stepped back. "It just doesn't feel right, breaking into someone's home."

"I agree. But we have to get warm. Let's explore."

He ran his hand along the wall by the door, searching for a light switch, found one and flipped it. Nothing happened.

"No electricity," he said. "Or it's turned off, but I don't really expect there is any on such a little island. Whoever owns this place probably has their own generator somewhere."

He shut the door, and slowly they moved into the shadowy interior of the house. Faint light coming through several uncurtained, oversized windows defined the perimeter of what seemed to be one very large room.

Tyler bumped into something hard with his elbow. "Ouch! What's this?"

He ran his hand along a ledge or shelf. "It's a cooking island or maybe a bar. Must be a kitchen area here. Maybe even some food," he added hopefully.

He could just make out the outlines of several tall stools aligned along the counter edge. He commandeered one to use as a makeshift walker. Scooting it along in front of him then leaning on it helped to take some of the weight off his aching, almost useless, leg and ankle as he dragged himself farther into the house.

April walked cautiously in front of him, her arms outstretched, searching for unseen obstacles.

"Here's a couch," she said, her hands patting a hulking lump in the middle of the floor. "Oh, and it's stacked with blankets and cushions and throws."

"Good." A wave of exhaustion washed over his shaking body, leaving him weak and dizzy. "I can't hold on much longer. Get out of your wet things. We'll dry off with one of the blankets and get under the rest."

He hoped it wasn't too late. His eyes had adjusted to the gloomy light, but somehow the room seemed to be getting steadily darker.

Leaning on the stool for support, he stripped off his soaking wet clothes as quickly as his trembling fingers could manage; but when he looked up, April hadn't moved. She stood on the other side of the couch, staring at him.

He felt a sharp pang. It hurt that, after all they'd shared, she would still feel uneasy over taking her clothes off in front of him. He'd lost so much with her, but it couldn't be helped. It was the way it had to be.

"April, please," he whispered. "We have to get dry and generate some body heat together. It's the only way. There's probably a heating system here, but we'd never find it and get it working in the dark."

He hobbled around the couch to where she stood. He struggled with her dripping clothes until, finally galvanized into action by his cold-induced clumsiness, she helped him pull them off. They tossed the wet things into a heap on the floor, and he bundled both their nude bodies into a fuzzy blanket. Tenderly, he rubbed her curls with a corner of the blanket, until her hair was almost dry, then they sank down on the huge couch and piled all the blankets and throws on top of them.

April nestled her back spoon-fashion against his chest. Tyler wrapped his arms and legs around her petite body. Gradually, their trembling calmed, as the mountain of blankets trapped the body heat generated by their shivering and slowly warmed them. Needles of pain danced along his skin as feeling returned to his nearly frozen extremities.

Exquisitely aware of the delicate curves of buttock and breast cuddled against his legs and arms, Tyler marveled at April's unconscious ability to arouse him in the most unlikely of circumstances. Even now, when he was almost surely unable to perform, he wanted her.

And what amazed him even more was how absolutely right she felt in his arms. As a final blanket of sleep warmed his exhausted, battered body, he uneasily realized he wished April could stay right where she was forever.

~ * ~

Tyler awakened to a blaze of sunlight. He squinted his eyes against the glare. The heat felt wonderful, licking at his face. He stretched his neck toward the light and basked in the glow like a contented cat as he reached for April.

She wasn't there. His spirits plummeted. Then, as he threw back the pile of covers and sat up, a divine odor penetrated his groggy senses. He sniffed like a bird dog as he looked around the cabin. Could he have died and gone to heaven, or was that really coffee?

Perched on a tall stool, sipping from an over-sized ceramic mug, April sat at the kitchen island he'd bumped into the previous night. Sunshine burnished her copper curls to a polished metallic gleam. Corkscrew tendrils still sprang from her head in wild abandon, but somehow, this morning the disarray had an artfully arranged look.

She was wrapped in a thick, blue terry-cloth robe at least four sizes too big for her; heavy, woodsman-type, gray wool socks puddled thickly around her slender ankles; and red scratches and purple bruises marred her otherwise perfect—if you didn't count a freckle or two—creamy, freshly scrubbed skin; but she still managed to look like a comfortable hausfrau at her morning koffee klatch.

Tyler blinked hard, trying to clear away this vision. It didn't compute. It didn't fit with all they'd been through— kidnappings and being chased through a wilderness by armed criminals. He must be dreaming or hallucinating.

She turned her head toward the couch and caught him staring at her.

"Good morning," she said cheerfully. "Would you like breakfast or a shower first?"

A dazed, "What?" that sounded more like duh? to his own ears was all he could manage for a response.

"The reconstituted powdered scrambled eggs aren't so hot, but the canned corned beef hash isn't half bad. And I made biscuits, too. There isn't any butter, but there's honey." She waved her mug at him. "And, of course, coffee."

Grimacing at the flare of pain, Tyler swung his legs over the side of the couch. He ran his hands through his tangled hair and scrubbed at his sand-and-salt-encrusted face, wincing at the cuts and bruises. "So how did you accomplish all these miracles?" he asked.

"It was easy in the daylight," she said airily. "It's all set up pretty much the way you figured. There's a generator run by bottled gas. The stove and water heater run on gas, too, and," she pointed at a huge stone hearth, where a small but cheery fire burned, "a fireplace for heat."

Her voice lost some of its confident briskness. "I couldn't find a telephone, though. Or even a TV or a radio. It's like you said, this place probably is someone's vacation home, a get-away-from-it-all kind of retreat."

Tyler sorted through the pile of blankets, picked a light knit throw decorated with black and white cows and tied it around his waist. Using the stool he'd left by the couch, he pulled himself up and shuffled over to the counter to join April. He couldn't decide whether he should be grumpy or grateful that she had accomplished so much while he slept.

She grinned mischievously at him, arching a copper-colored eyebrow at his tasteful breakfast attire. "I considered, for all of about thirty seconds, waiting for you to eat, but I was too starved."

She hopped down from her stool, and in a matter of minutes a plateful of the most delicious food he'd ever eaten magically appeared before him. He wanted to down the whole thing in one gulp like a ravening animal, but he forced himself to slowly fill his shrunken belly. He wrapped his hands around a steaming mug of strong coffee and blissfully breathed in the reviving fumes. "It's all wonderful, April. Somehow, I never thought you'd be a good cook."

"Are you kidding? My mother would never dream of letting anyone out of her house to get a place of their own, until they could pass the apple pie and biscuit examination."

He scraped the plate with his fork to get every last morsel then wiped his mouth with the paper napkin. "Well, thank your mother when you see her, and thank you. You saved my life."

She raised her cup to him. "And vice versa, several times over."

Swiveling on her stool, April pointed to a floor-to-ceiling wall of open shelves. "The pantry's well-stocked with food, actually. Lots of canned things and nonperishable staples like powered milk and flour and oil. We won't starve, at least not for a long time, but I can't see any way to get home."

She put her cup down, and he saw a small, involuntary shudder ripple across her face. "At least without swimming back to the bigger island first."

He didn't blame her for being afraid of the freezing water. He felt something like a shudder slither along his spine at the thought of getting back into those cold, black depths himself. But how soon would it be before Smith got a boat and sent a search party to their idyllic little Robinson Caruso hide-away?

Wanting to reassure her, he covered her hand with one of his. "Don't worry about that for now. We're warm and safe," he patted his stomach, "and full. That's all we have to be concerned with for the time being."

He felt her hand tremble. It felt so tiny and fragile under his large palm, and yet, he had seen her accomplish astonishing feats that a giant would be hard-pressed to manage.

Still, she seemed vulnerable to him now. He started to say something about his growing feelings for her, but as he opened his mouth, she shyly looked up into his face through her long lashes and burst out laughing. Stung, Tyler pulled his hand away.

She pointed at his face. "You may be full and warm, but you're sure not clean." She tried to stifle her giggles. "You should see your face. What a mess."

"All right," he said gruffly. "I get the message. Where's the shower?"

"Over there." She indicated a door opposite the kitchen. "And there's a sleeping loft with a great big closet full of clothes."

Tyler looked at the filthy, sodden heap of nearly shredded clothing lying on the floor. "I suppose we could use some replacements."

Her face dimpled. "Unfortunately, the owners of this cabin are slightly on the chubby side, but I think we can rig up new outfits, if we get creative with their belts."

She took his empty plate and cup and put them in the sink. "You can't climb up to the loft, so I'll pick some things out for you. While you're showering, I'll explore the island. Maybe somebody else lives here, or maybe I can find a boat. There's a dock in front of the cabin with a boardwalk leading all the way down to it. You can see it from the windows, but I haven't been down to the water yet."

Tyler's face twisted into a scowl. "I don't want you running all over the island by yourself. What if you have an accident, and I don't know where you are? Or what if Smith and his men find a way over here?" *Damn!* He hadn't intended to mention that.

He clenched his jaw at her sympathetic expression. She clearly regarded him as an invalid in need of her pity. "It can't be helped," she said. "You can't get around. I have to do it. I've thought about Smith, too. We have to find a way to get home—the sooner the better."

"But... "

It was too late. She was already scampering up the steep spiral metal stairway. In a few minutes a flurry of blue jeans and flannel shirts fluttered down to the floor, as she gaily tossed them over the loft railing.

In a few more minutes she came down herself, dressed in clothing that would make anyone else look like a clown, but on April they somehow managed to appear stylish. Tied into a knot with both ends hanging down, a worn leather belt held up faded jeans gathered into big pleats around her slender waist. Both the loden wool shirtsleeves and jeans cuffs were folded numerous times to shorten them to the right length.

Laughing at herself, she twirled in front of him, then plopped down on the floor, stuffed rolled up socks into the toes of a pair of hiking boots and laced them onto her feet. She got up and tried a few clumsy, shuffling steps around the room. She grimaced. "I guess these clodhoppers'll have to do, but I hope I don't have to outrun anything faster than a turtle."

She pulled on a gray and black patterned ski sweater that hung down to her knees, pushed up its sleeves and set a knit black beret at a jaunty angle on top of her riot of curls. She gave him a mocking salute and, without another word, clumped out of the house, shutting the door behind her.

Tyler swallowed a lump in his throat. It was foolish, even childish, but he felt abandoned. He knew he couldn't stop her, and it was beneath his dignity to beg, so he'd let her go, but it hurt. In spite of telling himself he couldn't afford to care for her, he'd let her get under his skin, and the pain he was feeling now was the predictable result.

He slammed his fist into the back of an over-stuffed chair. He hated this feeling of helplessness, of being out of control, of caring for someone who was bound to hurt him, was, in fact, hurting him right now.

He shuffled into the bathroom and, for the first time in his life, showered sitting down. The hot water felt wonderful; he wasn't sure he could ever get warm enough again. Even the sting of the water against his cuts and abrasions served a useful purpose. It helped a little to take his mind off April.

Once out of the shower he discovered the roomy bathroom was well stocked with clean towels, toiletries, disinfectants and Band-Aids—even new, still-in-their-containers toothbrushes.

The toothbrush April had used lay in a little puddle of water on the vanity top next to a mangled tube of toothpaste with the cap off. Her damp towel dangled crookedly from the towel rack.

Tyler wiped up the water, replaced the cap, straightened the tube, folded the towel and hung it neatly on the rack, wondering what it would be like to share a bathroom with April for always.

He grinned. More than likely she'd try to spice up his life by stocking the bathtub with frogs or maybe even alligators. He'd probably go crazy in a week.

After treating his wounds with antiseptic and wrapping his ankle with elastic bandages from the bathroom medicine cabinet, Tyler sorted through the clothing April had thrown down to the living room floor.

She was right; the owners of the vacation house must be chubby, but they couldn't be too tall. She'd had to roll up the clothes to fit her because she was so tiny. He needed a belt to keep the jeans up, but the bottom of the pants hit him mid-calf, and the shirtsleeves only came to the middle of his forearms. He caught a glimpse of himself in a mirror and laughed aloud. Somehow, he didn't look as stylish in his borrowed clothes as April had.

His laugh turned to a frown, as he wondered where she was and what she was doing right now. The way she dashed off without thinking things through drove him wild. What if something happened to her while he was stuck here, helpless in the cabin, unable to do anything about it? He hated being the weak link in a team.

He sat down on the couch but couldn't remain still. Restlessly, he started shaking out, folding and stacking the blankets they had slept under, memories of the way she'd felt in his arms torturing him. He squeezed his hands into fists, crushing the wool between his fingers. He really thought she might drive him to madness.

He was accustomed to being in charge of himself and those around him. He didn't mind taking suggestions from others. In fact, in his business he welcomed intelligent advice, but he expected to make the final decision after giving a problem a lot of thought and making a careful plan.

He gave the last blanket an especially hard shake before folding it and adding it to the pile. He absolutely never charged into a situation without first thinking it through. He might not do the actual work himself, but he damn sure wanted to control the organizing and delegating.

April never gave him a chance to delegate anything. She was always off and running, before he'd even formulated the schedule.

Tyler closed his eyes, put his head back against the back of the couch and tried to relax his tense muscles. He knew he should elevate his feet and not risk any further injury, but he just couldn't lie there, when April had already accomplished so much today.

Using his stool/walker to get around, he rinsed out what was left of their own clothing and hung them on the cabin's deck railing to dry. Anxiously, he scanned the landscape around the house, searching for April, but there was no sign of her. Just an endless vista of trees and ocean, very beautiful but not what he wanted to see.

Muttering to himself, he went back inside and sat on his stool to wash the dishes. Then he heated a can of soup, fervently hoping April would be back soon to eat it with him.

Just as he finished setting the counter for two, April burst in through the door. She seemed to bring in sunshine and fresh air with her. He thought maybe he even heard some kind of music, as she entered the room, but surely that was only birdsong and wind stirring through the pines outside.

But she'd come back. She'd returned to him. Rationally, he'd been reasonably certain she would in spite of the real dangers that stalked them; but emotionally, he reluctantly admitted to himself, he'd been dead sure he'd never see her again. Now he couldn't prevent his heart from leaping with joy at the sight of her.

"So, what did you find?" he asked as calmly as he could, trying not to show how relieved he was at her return.

She threw the beret and sweater onto a chair and slumped down on a stool at the counter. "Not a thing. It's really a tiny little island. I went all the way around it. I'll bet whoever built this cabin owns the whole thing. There aren't any other houses, and there aren't any boats. And there weren't any signs of life on what I could see of the other islands from here, either."

She raised her head and sniffed. "Something smells good." When she realized he was ladling out soup, she jumped up and rushed over to the stove. "Sit down this instant," she scolded. "You shouldn't be on your feet anymore than you absolutely have to be. I'll do that."

He sat down at the counter, and April served up the chicken noodle soup and crackers and canned peaches.

"We might be able to make a crude raft if there are any tools around," Tyler said between slurps of hot soup. "Or at the very least we could hold onto a log for support as we swim or maybe use one as a kind of surfboard."

"Maybe."

Tyler watched her swirl the last of her soup around the bottom of the bowl. She seemed uncharacteristically reluctant to think about their escape from the island. He would have expected her to have already thrown herself into the sea.

Her face brightened. "I didn't see any tools, but I did find fishing gear." She paused dramatically. "And guess what else?"

"I can't guess, April," he said grouchily.

She jumped down from the stool and charged out of the house, calling back to him over her shoulder. "I'll show you."

In a few minutes she was back with a fishing pole in one hand and pulling a good-sized red wagon with the other. It rattled and clattered behind her across the hardwood floor. "See!" she said. "Island transportation. I'll bet they use it to bring supplies and stuff along the boardwalk up from their boat."

She dropped the handle of the wagon and darted over to tug at his sleeve. "But I figure we can use it to haul you down to the dock, so we can catch something for supper."

Her face took on a pleading expression. "Please, Tyler. Let's just rest today. We can think about getting off the island tomorrow."

He knew they should be plotting out a course of action, but she seemed to be tugging at his heart as much as his shirtsleeve. He longed to give in to her spontaneous spirit of fun. He hesitated but couldn't resist her plea. Then, once he gave up on his sense of responsibility, it was easy to give up his dignity as well and submit to looking ridiculous perched in the red wagon.

They fished companionably all afternoon. April shrieked like a Banshee every time they caught a fish and danced all over the dock, while he unhooked them. Tyler couldn't remember the last time he'd had so much fun. As another glorious sunset set the sky aflame, April trundled him back up to the cabin. He gutted the fish, and she fried them to perfection.

In spite of April's protests that he was overtaxing his injured legs, they cleaned the kitchen up together then sat in front of a blazing fire, soaking up the heat.

It seemed only natural to pull her into his arms. She rested her head against his shoulder, and he nuzzled his chin in her fragrant, soft curls. He felt as though he were being torn apart, his brain at war with his body. If he were to draw up a balance sheet listing the pros and cons of caring for April, he could think of a dozen things to list on the con side and only one on the pro—he wanted her.

He dropped a kiss on the tickly little hairs at the nape of her neck and, even with such a simple act, felt his blood roar through his body. How could anything that exciting, that made him feel so alive, be so wrong for him?

He was fairly sure April felt a similar kind of confusion. This morning she'd been hell bent on getting off the island; by afternoon she'd seemed content to postpone their escape indefinitely.

As his lips smoothed across the delicate curve of her neck, he heard a soft moan. She raised her head and stared into his eyes, her own glowing with an emotion he couldn't—wouldn't—define. Her soft, rosy lips were slightly parted. To protest?

He didn't give her a chance to say anything. He lowered his head and captured her mouth, gently at first, then when she didn't withdraw, he let loose the tight rein he'd kept on his emotions. He savaged her lips, her teeth, her tongue, thrusting, sucking, biting. She responded with a wildness as great as his own.

They stripped one another's clothing away, kissing and biting flesh, as it was exposed. There was no hesitation, no doubts or confusion now. They acted as one. He ripped into her soft, wet, coral petals of flesh and roared out as sensations he'd never felt, or even thought possible, overcame him. She raged along with him, her cries ringing into the night with his. Her feet and legs, her nails and hands, her lips and teeth seemed to touch his body everywhere at once. They bucked and heaved and tumbled and twisted, until their pleasure reached a crescendo so intense it might have been pain. Tyler crashed down from another world, a place he'd never been before.

Dazed, overcome with emotions he'd never known existed, unable to think or analyze, Tyler lay curled close to April, panting, stroking, murmuring, until sleep finally claimed them.

Thirteen

April woke up to sun pouring in the windows. She sighed. It must already be after eight a.m. She checked her watch. Yep. 8:20. Amazing it still worked after all they'd been through. Old reliable. Like Tyler. She lay nestled next to him, his arms and legs curled around her, protecting her even in sleep. They had never gotten up from the blankets in front of the fireplace where they'd made love last night. The fire was out now, but she still felt warm and cozy next to Tyler, lying under and on top of the piles of blankets.

What a night! She'd never dreamed making love could even approach the feelings she'd had. No wonder so many books and movies were devoted to the subject. She should have put sex at the top of her list when she'd first left home, determined to have as many new and different adventures as she could before she became old and decrepit, instead of waiting around so long before she tried it.

Still, she thought the intensity of the experience just might have something to do specifically with Tyler and the fact that she'd fallen hopelessly in love with him. She doubted if she could duplicate those emotions with just any old Joe she might pick up on a street corner. If only she and Tyler could keep at it forever. She sighed again. But they couldn't.

She nudged Tyler's chest with her elbow. "Wake up, slug-about. Time's awasting."

He stirred against her. A lovely hardness pulsed against her thighs. She hoped he'd been dreaming about her.

"We can't wait any longer. We have to do something today. Got to get off the island and find the police," April said.

Tyler yawned and stretched his arms out of the covers and up over their heads. He rubbed his sleep-dazed eyes then propped himself up on one elbow. "You have any ideas?"

"Not yet, but I will." She bunched her muscles, preparing for the shock of the cold morning outside their warm nest of blankets, then dashed around the room, collecting her strewn-everywhere clothes, pulling each item on haphazardly as soon as she found it.

Tyler chuckled, as she hopped on one foot, trying to pull the too-long pants up far enough on her other leg to roll the cuff high enough to walk.

But by the time she was fully dressed, he seemed to have sobered considerably. "You're right, April, we've already wasted way too much time."

Oh, that hurt! Yesterday might very well have been her finest hour, their lovemaking capping every hiking/biking experience she'd ever had. She knew they had to find a way off the island, that's why she had given him a wake-up call, but how could he call their day together a waste of time? Though he was right, of course; it really had been silly of her to give into her desire just to be with him.

"Right," she said gruffly, straining not to let the pain come through in her voice. "What day is it? I've kind of lost track of the time."

"Let's see. Willis and Harmon grabbed us Friday. We spent that night in the cave. The next day, Saturday, is when we landed on this island and broke into the cabin. We slept here last night, too, that would have been Sunday, so today's Monday."

He looked at her with an expression she couldn't decipher. "We've packed a lot into those three days, haven't we, April?"

"Yep, a lot," her voice still tight. "So, it's Monday morning. I don't think XPress is going to do much but grumble when I don't show up, but probably a lot of people will be expecting you. Do you think anyone's looking for us yet? What will your staff do when you don't arrive right on the dot of whenever you're supposed to be there?"

Tyler raised a dark brow. "'Right on the dot?' Do I detect a note of sarcasm, April?"

"Who, me? Sarcastic? I just can't imagine you being late for any scheduled event. And that's a good thing, at least for us right now. Really, were you supposed to be at your office this morning? Is somebody looking for you?"

"Let me think about it. I don't have my planner with me, naturally, but I'm sure I can remember what was scheduled for today if I give it some thought. Rita, my executive assistant, usually keeps me on track, but yes, I check the schedule myself pretty often. I just can't believe it's already Monday."

Tyler pushed back the blankets and stood up. April looked away hastily. He must have been dreaming about somebody! She didn't think that, even if she were treated to the sight of Humanoid erectus Tylerous every morning for the rest of her life, she'd ever get used to the staggering spectacle of Tyler's uncovered equipment. He moved around the room with the help of his chair/walker, apparently unconcerned with his nudity, gathering his clothing, then took his things into the bathroom.

April sighed again. She seemed to remember Tyler doing a lot of that when she'd first met him. He must have passed it on to her.

But sighing wasn't going to change anything. It never helped the lovelorn heroines in books like *Wuthering Heights*, and it wouldn't help her. Action is what she prided herself on, and action is what would work now.

She went into the kitchen and put a saucepan of oatmeal and water on the stove to cook then rummaged in the pantry until she found brown sugar, canned milk and raisins to make it into a more palatable breakfast. She had just finished filling the coffee maker, when Tyler hobbled out of the bathroom, looking freshly scrubbed in his too-small clothes.

"My turn," April said.

When she came out of the bathroom, Tyler was sitting at the counter, spooning up oatmeal and raisins as though it were ambrosia and drinking a mug of steaming coffee.

"I poured you a cup," he said.

She perched on one of the bar stools next to him and sipped the hot coffee. He had sugared it exactly the way she liked it! She wrapped both hands around the mug for the warmth and looked speculatively at him over the rim. *Could he possibly be one of those rare trainable men?* She sighed. *Probably not in any area that really matters.*

"I though about what my schedule was supposed to be today," he said, "and I had planned to start out at the office. I get there early when I go in first thing. I live in a condo in Belltown, one of my firm's designs," the pride ringing strong in his voice, "so I don't have a commute. I imagine Rita has already tried calling me at home and my cell. She'd think something was wrong as soon as she arrived at the office and saw that I wasn't there. I always beat her in when I'm scheduled to start the day at the office."

"Surprise, surprise," April muttered.

Tyler grinned at her. "I don't know why you always look like you've bitten into a lemon every time I mention the word 'schedule.' As I recall, the very first time I met you, you gave me a lecture on how I was wasting your clients' time. That was the lecture that followed you slugging me with the blueprint tube."

"Which I lost," she said glumly.

That crack wiped some of the early-morning chipperness off his face.

"It couldn't be helped," he said softly. "We'll get Smith without them."

He was silent for a few minutes, pretending to concentrate on his oatmeal when he was probably really thinking about what an idiot she was, who couldn't even hang on to a crucial piece of evidence.

"So," he finally continued, "I don't know what Rita would do next. She might call around to the foremen at some of our active sites to see if I were at any of them, but I always let her know where I am, so I'm pretty sure she'd think that was useless. She would be worried, I know, but I don't believe she'd think to call the police right away. And I don't know much about how they work, except from the dubious knowledge gained from movies, but isn't there a forty-eight hour thing? You know, the police won't look for someone, or even allow a missing person's report, until forty-eight hours have gone by."

"Someone might have seen Willis and Harmon snatch us and reported it."

"Maybe, at least for you. I noticed a couple of people in cars watching pretty closely what was going on when Harmon picked you up. You looked terrible, hanging out of those hammy arms of his."

A violent spasm clenched Tyler's face. For a moment his calm businessman's facade turned into something brutal. He made a visible effort to regain control. "I doubt if anyone saw me since I was dumb enough to let them lure me into an alley. But the real point is, I don't think it makes any difference what Rita or some good-Samaritan observer or even the police do. Again, I don't know much about how the police work, but I can't see how there'd be any way to trace us up here. At least not in a few days. Not unless Jim Stolz got away and contacted them."

"So, if no one is looking for us here in the islands, we need to attract some attention." She jumped down from the stool. "I'll go build a bonfire on the beach. Then if any boats go by, maybe someone will investigate, and *voilà*, we'll be rescued." She started for the door.

"April! Wait! Don't go running off like that without thinking it through. First of all, there's a house and a dock here. Any boater seeing a bonfire would just think it was someone enjoying their vacation place."

"So? I'll build a really big bonfire, one nobody could ignore. Or even better, maybe I can spell out 'SOS' with branches or make something else to attract attention." She turned toward the door again.

"April!"

How he managed to put so much exasperation into a two-syllable name, her name, a perfectly fine name, she couldn't imagine.

"What?" She tried to sound as fed-up as he had.

"Aren't you forgetting something else?"

She shrugged. There were about a million other things to consider, but she thought it was time to just go ahead and pick a course of action and get on with it.

"Smith. You do remember him, don't you? Anything you do to attract the attention of someone who might or might not be passing by is a whole lot more likely to announce our presence to the one person who does know about where we are, or were, and who actually cares."

"But he doesn't know there wasn't any way to get off this island. He probably thinks we're home by now and have already talked to the police. He's probably putting together an alibi or a defense of some kind; maybe he's even leaving the country. Crooks do that if they have lots of money, don't they?"

He shook his head. She could see him silently tut-tutting at her naïveté, before he actually spoke. "April, that's just wishful thinking.

He wants us totally out of the picture; he's not going to leave anything to chance. He had plenty of time to check our homes yesterday. He'll check us out at our workplaces this morning. When he finds out neither of us are where we're supposed to be, the next logical thing for him to do would be to rent or charter a boat and comb the little islands along the shore of the bigger island we swam from."

He got off the stool and used it to move a few steps in one direction then a couple of steps back the other way. He'd obviously be pacing the length of the room while he thought out loud if he had full command of his legs. She didn't think he even knew she was still in the room.

"Hopefully," he continued, "the guys who shot at us can't pick out this island right away, especially approaching it from the sea, but we definitely can't count on that. There's any number of ways they could have marked the coast of the big island, or maybe they're just really familiar with the whole area. It might be as easy for them to find this island as it would be for us locate two intersecting street corners in Seattle. In any case, no matter whether they're familiar with the islands or not, lighting a bonfire or making some kind of a sign could bring them right to us."

"So, what you're saying sounds like there isn't anything we can do. We've already decided there isn't any way to get off the island except for swimming, and we agreed we don't want to try that. If we can't attract attention, what else is there to do besides just waiting around to see if Smith is going to come? I don't want to be a sitting duck; I want to do something." She smacked her clenched fist into the palm of her hand in frustration and for emphasis.

"I didn't say we couldn't do anything. I just don't think we've come up with a sound plan yet. And I definitely don't want you dashing around getting us into more trouble."

"Oh! You! Me—more trouble!" she sputtered.

"Okay, I shouldn't have said that. You're not the one who got us into this mess. You're actually more or less an innocent bystander."

"That's more like it," she sniffed, only slightly mollified. It was so easy to tell what he really thought of her. Troublemaker. The problem, not the problem solver.

"So, what do you think of this? We build a bonfire or a sign, but at the same time we figure out something to do if Smith is the one to see it."

"Like what? I don't see any AK-47s lying around here. We already looked for weapons."

"Well... maybe surprise, stealth. Bushes grow right up to the water by the dock. We could conceal ourselves in the bushes. I'm assuming most of Smith's men would get off the boat to look for us onshore. And equally sure he'd leave at least one or two to guard the boat. If we could slip into the water and swim to the boat without the guards seeing us, and if it's possible to climb into the boat quickly, we might be able to overpower whomever he leaves behind."

"Yes!" April shouted. Now he was talking. Something they could do instead of standing around gabbing.

He clumped the stool over to the couch and dropped down on it in an attitude of discouragement. He ran his fingers through his thick, dark hair, dropped his head back to rest on the top of the couch and spoke to the beams under the roof of the building. "Way too many 'ifs.' It's a Hollywood scenario—Castaway meets Rambo. How could we actually climb into a boat and surprise killers with guns? It's a script for getting killed. Not to mention the logistics. Like what if no one comes here for days or even weeks—Smith or anyone else? How long can we huddle in a clump of bushes? What about food? Sleep? No, it's ridiculous to even think that way."

"No, it isn't." April ran over to the couch, plopped down beside him and grabbed his hands. "It's a good plan; we just need to fine-tune it a little. We take food to the hiding place, obviously. We take turns sleeping and watching. We increase our odds of surprising anyone on the boat by, say... swimming under water. Right! That would work. I saw plastic straws in the pantry. We could use them like snorkels to breath under the water."

He smiled indulgently at her, condescendingly. "So, now we've added Steve McQueen in *Papillon* to our screenplay?"

"No way. He used hollow reeds, as I recall; we've got plastic. Much more high-tech. So, maybe straws wouldn't work; I don't know. The point is we're heading in the right direction. We're coming up with something better than sitting around here wringing our hands and making endless, perfect plans. This is something we can actually go and do right now. Implement a plan. That's probably a business-kind-of-word you'd like."

She jumped up off the couch and headed once more for the door. "I'm going to scout the bushes next to the dock. See if there's really enough of them to give us cover. Maybe I can dig a little foxhole sort of thing underneath. Give us more room."

"Wait, April! Wait for me. I'll come with you." He hauled himself up from the couch, hanging onto his stool/walker.

She stuck her tongue out at him. No use in being too serious, when it was only your lives that were at stake. "You're too slow. But you can look in the pantry, get some food ready for us to take to our hideout."

She slipped along the splintery wooden path that led to the dock, already feeling stealthy, even in her too-big shoes, getting into the role.

The dock was long, reaching out far into the water. A good-sized boat could probably moor beside it; the water was sure to be deep that far from shore. Great clumps of salal, hardhack and Oregon grape grew almost to the waterline. Oregon grape's spiny leaves resembled holly and would be equally prickly if they tried to nestle down underneath the branches. Maybe they could just crouch behind the shrubs. With the dock going out so far over the water, perhaps they really could hide under it with the straw snorkels. Hide behind bushes, slip into the water in the shadows under the dock when they saw a boat coming, then either attack if the sailors turned out to be Smith's gang or jubilantly greet their rescuers if they weren't.

Tyler had called their plans Hollywood. Maybe the way they were thinking was insane. But what else was there to do? Enough food for maybe a week or two was stored in the pantry, if they weren't too piggy with their meals. As attractive as the idea of playing house with Tyler for a few weeks was, it surely wasn't any more sensible to sit around and wait for someone to find them than to try to attract attention and prepare for the possibility of an attack. They had to think Hollywood. Movies were about extraordinary circumstances, and that's what they were in.

But nothing would be accomplished, if she continued to stand around mulling over their situation. Action! That's what she needed. Time to stop thinking and start doing.

She trotted away from the dock and started pulling big pieces of driftwood into a pile. Sign or bonfire, these branches and logs would work. Many of the giant trees, scoured and polished to a silver sheen by the sea, were far too heavy for her to move, but there were smaller bits scattered along the coast. Plenty to meet her goal.

~ * ~

Tyler watched April lugging branches bigger than she was to a central location a dozen or so yards from the dock. He smiled wryly. She'd taken his dreaming-aloud suggestions at face value and was busily making them real. He wondered what kind of palace she'd managed to construct under the shrubs by the dock.

He turned away from the window and hobbled back toward the kitchen where he'd loaded the little red wagon with cans of food that, if they weren't too particular, could be eaten cold. He was going along with the fantasy since he couldn't think of anything better to do.

Tyler winced as he unsuccessfully tried to move across the floor with the barstool without putting any weight on his worst leg. He hadn't wanted April to know just how bad his legs ached. He was fairly certain that something was broken in one leg, and his ankle, even if it wasn't actually broken, was swelling alarmingly and hurt like hell. He felt flushed and hot even though he was pretty sure it was cool to cold in the cabin, since they hadn't lit a fire yet today. A fever? Did that mean he had an infection or blood poisoning from a broken bone? He was already practically useless for April; he fervently hoped he didn't get any worse.

Though he was exceedingly grateful that at least one part of his anatomy still worked just fine. He closed his eyes for a moment the better to remember their night of passionate lovemaking. Never had sex been so good.

He'd been surprised when April woke him up and seemed so determined to get off the island today. She had been the one the day before who had wanted to slow down and enjoy the day.

Tyler frowned. Maybe he hadn't actually been such a great lover after all.

He banged the stool down hard against the floor, exasperated at his uncharacteristic lack of confidence. April caused him to play weird games with his head, but he couldn't be wrong about the perfection of the night. She had enjoyed their bodies just as much as he had.

Maybe she was just getting tired of him already. That seemed much, much more likely. "Okay, been there, done that, time to move on," just like she did with her jobs.

He grabbed a coil of clothesline rope out of the pantry. No more second-guessing April. It was a sure way to drive himself crazy. Better to try to be useful, no matter how much he hurt, no matter if it was in service of a harebrained scheme.

Experimentally, he tied the wagon handle to the crossbars of the stool. If he straddled the cord, maybe he could pull the wagon along behind him to the dock. He moved slowly, awkwardly, across the cabin toward the door that led to the path to the dock, lifting the stool and setting it down, shuffling his aching feet and legs along behind it. The wagon rolled erratically along with him, occasionally picking up too much speed and banging into his calves. So what was one more little twinge? At least he was doing something more or less useful.

As he made his way painfully along the plank-paved trail, he watched April bound from the pile of wood to another log, lug it back and throw it up on what had become a gigantic mound of tangled branches. She paused to wipe the sleeve of her shirt across her forehead then dug in her pocket and pulled something out. She moved out of his line of vision behind the mountain of wood. He saw a small red glow flare up through the latticework of branches, then April moved to the side of the pile where she stood, hands on hips, arms akimbo, seemingly admiring her handiwork.

His muscles clenched involuntarily. *Damn it, no!* They weren't supposed to light a signal fire until they were hidden. It was a stupid idea even at that, but better than standing out in the open shouting, "Hey, Smith, here we are! Come and get us!"

He tried to move faster to get to April, tried to get her attention by shouting, but she didn't hear him. In what seemed like a matter of moments, the small blaze turned into a raging inferno the size of a Montana forest fire.

Finally, April heard his yells. She waved at him then came tearing up the path toward him, her face split wide in a gorgeous grin.

Even before she reached him, she began babbling in a torrent of happy pride. "Isn't it beautiful? I couldn't wait; I wanted to see it burn. I can make another one. Isn't it huge? Isn't it great? I love it!"

He opened his mouth to scold her, to tell her how foolish she was behaving, but shut it with a snap, as she barreled into him, hugging him hard around the middle, almost knocking him off his feet. He grimaced in pain, but in spite of himself his lips twisted into a reluctant smile. *What's the use? Nothing will change April. Why bother to even try?*

He clutched the stool with one hand, trying to hang onto his equilibrium, and hugged her back with his other arm, bending over to bury his face in her fragrant blaze of copper curls, which were ever bit as bright as the gigantic bonfire.

She raised her face to him, and he kissed her, a kiss so sweet it made him tremble. "April, oh April, what am I going to do with you?" he murmured, until a noise buzzing along the edges of his consciousness became so loud it engaged his attention.

He looked up and, without thought, pulled her closer to him. "Look. A boat. It's coming this way. Maybe your signal fire worked."

She broke away and ran toward the dock. "Wait, April!" he screamed. "We need to be careful. It could be... "

But she was already standing at the end of the dock, waving a fishing pole they'd failed to put away yesterday, to signal the boat, though it clearly was heading straight toward them. She put one hand to her brow to shade her eyes from the glare of the sun and turned to him.

"Tyler, I don't have a good feeling about this." She swung back toward the ocean to squint at the rapidly approaching powerboat. "Doesn't that man in the bow look kind of like... "

She gasped, pounded back along the dock to where he was and raced off into the trees that grew almost up to the wide wooden planks.

"April! What the... "

But he knew. What they had feared all along had now happened. Smith had returned.

Tyler looked back at the boat. One of the crew had jumped to the dock to secure the vessel. He pulled the boat in until it scraped against the pilings, so Smith could alight with his usual composure. Inexorably, he closed the distance between himself and Tyler, gun at the ready.

Tyler felt utterly helpless. He had no weapon, couldn't run or swim away and was dead certain he couldn't talk himself out of danger. Hobbling away with his chair at a snail's pace was beneath his dignity and futile.

So, April had finally had enough sense to get away, while it was still possible. He only hoped she could find a secure hiding place on the tiny island. With his head he thanked God she had escaped, but unreasonably, his heart ached. Ultimately, when the final chips were down, she'd abandoned him.

Smith was only a few feet away now. "So," he said, raising the gun to point directly at Tyler's head, "the merry chase is over."

Tyler straightened his back, waiting. Would he hear the retort of the gun, feel the impact of the bullet? Would he register pain, or would there only be instant oblivion?

A tiny stirring in the branches overhead caused him to glance up involuntarily. *God, no!* He jerked his gaze back to Smith, as a hideous grimace split his face. He hoped Smith thought it was caused by fear for his own life.

April was crawling out on a thick branch overhead, clutching her fishing pole in one hand. In the split second when she'd realized he'd seen her, she'd grinned impishly at him and brandished the pole.

The woman is totally stark-raving mad, certifiable. And he was going to have to stand here and watch the woman he loved die.

He couldn't stand it. He hated her for putting him through this unbearable torture and hated himself for somehow falling in love with her.

He couldn't save her, but he could put off the inevitable for a few seconds. At least he would die first so he wouldn't have to witness her death.

Just as he bunched his muscles to spring at Smith, April swung the fishing pole. The heavy reel hit Smith square in the face. The gun went off, as Smith went down. Tyler felt an excruciating, searing pain tear through his arm. It hung limply at his side, but he threw the chair to one side and leaped on Smith. Using his good arm, he smashed him again and again until he had the supreme satisfaction of watching Smith's eyes roll up in his head and consciousness fade away.

At the blast of the gun, men had begun to pour off the boat. Then another sound filled the air—the dull beat, beat, beat of a helicopter overhead. Instantly, with much shouting and cursing, the crew reversed directions and scrambled frantically, almost comically, back on the boat.

"Police!" he heard roaring down over the drone of the helicopter blades in a strange voice-of-God amplified sound.

Tyler slid off Smith's inert body and lay gazing up at April, the beautiful little tree sprite who had saved their lives with her maniacal bravery.

It was all over now. The helicopter would take them away.

A pain greater than the broken leg or the gunshot wound ripped through him. How could he stand to live without April?

"Damn you, April," he muttered. "Damn you for making me care."

Fourteen

For the third time April nervously riffled through every hanger in her closet. She knew it was foolish to care so much, but she absolutely had to look perfect for her day in court. She wanted to be a credible witness when she testified against Smith, but that wasn't the most important reason that she had to make her appearance in style.

She held a floral print dress up to her body and looked in the mirror. *Wrong! All wrong.* Disgusted, she threw the dress on top of the mounting pile on her narrow bed.

For all intents and purposes Tyler had disappeared from her life. She hadn't seen or heard from him in months. Not since the police had helicoptered them to the hospital, thanks to Jim Stolz reporting them missing after he escaped from Smith. Ironically, Willis had been a patient in the same hospital but, fortunately, on a different floor and under police guard. Tyler's diversion had been successful, though Willis had been seriously wounded. According to what Jim Stolz had told her while they were waiting outside Tyler's hospital room, Harmon had rescued Willis. In the mass confusion following the mini-avalanche caused by Tyler's accurate pitch, Harmon had simply picked up the unconscious Willis, carried him to Tyler's Lexus and driven him straight to the hospital.

As happy as April was both that she and Tyler had probably saved the men's lives and that the two of them were currently awaiting trial in jail, it didn't make up for the pain she felt over missing Tyler. It seemed like an eternity, since she and Tyler had been together.

She sighed and sank down on the quilt next to the pile of clothes. Gingerly, she touched her chest. It hurt, almost as though her heart had been physically bruised. It had felt that way ever since she'd said goodbye to Tyler at the hospital after her night of observation. She'd known she was okay all along, and the doctors had finally condescended to agree with her. At least she was okay until she'd seen Tyler's dark skin and hair lying in stark contrast against the blindingly white hospital linens.

He'd barely said two words to her. The nurse in attendance was the one who'd cheerfully let her know the bullet had passed cleanly through his shoulder without doing any major, lasting damage and that he had a fractured tibia and a severely sprained ankle. She'd tried to kiss his cheek, but he'd turned his head away. The peculiar ache in her chest had begun then and showed no signs of ever going away.

She'd tried calling him a few times at his office. Surely, she had a right to inquire about his recovery after all they'd been through together, but his excessively protective assistant had taken so long examining his schedule, trying to find a moment when the busy Mr. Nielsen might possibly fit in a return call, she'd just given up. You'd think he was the head of a nation the way his assistant monitored his time. April certainly wasn't going to beg to talk to him.

Gnashing her teeth, she jumped up from the bed, grabbed a pants suit from the closet, cursorily inspected it and tossed it on the floor. She hating caring so much. How could one man cause so much pain? How could she have fallen in love so hard, so quickly, with a totally inappropriate, control-freak, schedule-bound, boring, stuffy, old businessman?

There must be something seriously wrong with her. A defect in her emotions gene. Mutations in the part of her DNA that was responsible for love and romance.

Yanking off the oversized Tweetie Bird tee shirt she'd slept in, April decided to wear her very best emerald-green silk suit. No matter what was wrong with her on the inside, she was determined for Tyler to see her today on the outside as a sophisticated, professional woman.

Today no mud splatters, sweat, rips, too-big clown clothes or bruises were allowed. Disastrous as falling in love with a man who couldn't love her back had been, she was determined, at least for today, no matter what the cost, to hold her head high and keep her dignity intact. She would make him regret, if only for a moment, what he had so casually rejected.

She jumped into the shower and furiously slapped on her highest-octane facial scrub, then ferociously lathered her hair with her top-gun shampoo. She would make him want her. Even if it killed her.

~ * ~

"Mr. Nielsen!" Tyler's executive assistant exclaimed in a shocked voice as she bustled into his office. "You haven't touched your monthly planner."

Tyler swung his chair away from the view of Elliot Bay and the Olympic Mountains and rolled back to his desk in one smooth whoosh. "Sorry, Rita, I guess it slipped my mind."

She stared at him as though he'd suddenly sprouted wings or grown horns.

"Don't worry about it," he said airily, "I'll get around to it eventually."

Narrowing her eyes, she planted her hands on her ample hips and looked him up and down. "I hope you haven't forgotten you have to testify today. I blocked out almost the whole day for court."

Tyler's heart speeded up at the thought. As if he could forget! In only a few hours he would see April. He swallowed the lump in his throat. To hide his excitement from Rita's eagle eyes, he stretched across his desk to pick up the stack of magazines he'd bought at the Pike Place Market magazine stand the day before.

"... hope they put that Ron Smith in jail and throw away the key," Rita was saying indignantly. "To think he'd jeopardize your vacation resort, after you'd worked so hard to make it perfect. Not to mention that Willis and Harmon. Imagine, they actually kidnapped you!"

He flipped through one of the magazines. "Don't worry, Rita," he said absent-mindedly. "With all the evidence Jim Stolz had spirited away from Smith's office and with what I added, the district attorney has a really strong case. And whenever Willis and Harmon's cases get scheduled, after Jim Stolz, April and I testify, they're bound to get put away almost as long as Smith will."

He held up a picture of a tiny boat slashing between huge boulders through a wall of boiling waves and spray. "Have you ever been kayaking? It looks exciting, don't you think? I've been thinking of giving it a try."

Rita's mouth dropped open. With the ease of a long and comfortable working relationship, she walked over to him and put her hand on his forehead. "You have to be running a temperature," she muttered. "There's got to be something seriously wrong with you."

A few hours later Tyler decided Rita might have been right after all. Though he'd only begun to feel feverish a minute ago. Not to mention dizzy, weak and his heart just might have gone into a fatal fibrillation. All at the sight of April striding purposefully down the courthouse hall.

He had to look twice to be sure it was really April. She looked like a movie-queen version of a career woman, a miniature but high-powered professional. And beautiful! Absolutely knock-dead gorgeous in a lustrous suit the exact same shade as her eyes. He tried unsuccessfully to suck in a lungful of air.

It was the way she walked that convinced him it was really April. No one else that small could ever cover ground the way April could. And in high-heeled black pumps, yet.

He wasn't sure exactly how he'd expected her to look. Of course, she wouldn't wear bike shorts and a helmet to testify in court, but somehow he'd expected more of the wild woodland sprite to shine through.

Not that this was bad. Oh no, not at all. The slippery fabric of her suit slithered over her delicate curves in a way that made all of his muscles tense as tightly as when they'd raced through the forest together. And the short skirt and high heels showed off her perfect legs to great advantage.

It was just that this new, unexpected April confused him. The carefully composed speech he'd crafted had flown right out of his head. He hadn't the foggiest recollection of what he'd intended to say. All he could think about was how wonderful it would feel to run his fingers through her artfully arranged copper curls, until they blazed out all around her head the way he remembered them in glorious, unruly abandon.

Still, as he approached her a little more cautiously than he'd originally planned, he couldn't manage to wipe the idiot grin off of his face; he was so happy to see her again.

But as he opened his mouth and his arms to greet her, she sailed right past him, chin high, eyes straight ahead, as though he weren't even there.

His mouth sagged in disbelief.

He spun on his heel, caught up with her in two hard strides and grabbed her arm. "What's this all about, April? After all we shared, you're just going to ignore me?"

She brushed at his hand as though it were a pesky gnat, until he released her. "'All we shared' was several months ago, as I recall. I might ask who's doing the ignoring. I might ask, that is, if I cared."

She stepped to one side to walk around him, but he moved to block her way. He tried to speak as though he were the one in charge, but even to his own ears, his voice came out sounding a trifle abject.

"I'm sorry I haven't called you, but I've been doing a lot of thinking since then. That's part of what I want to talk to you about now. I thought we could have dinner together tonight and discuss it."

He remembered how she had ecstatically eaten the PowerBar, when it was all they'd had. He could hardly wait to see what she'd do with steak and lobster.

She whipped an electronic calendar out of her portfolio briefcase and coolly punched in a few numbers. "So sorry. I'm booked for tonight. You really should have consulted me before you planned a meeting. I hope your assistant can rearrange your schedule without too much trouble."

Each word hit him with the frigid, hard sharpness of an ice cube. After she'd dumped the whole tray right on his unsuspecting head, she whisked past him and marched down the hall and out of his life forever.

~ * ~

April straddled her bike and fastened the strap of her helmet securely under her chin. Funny, how the simplest little thing seemed to take so much effort these days. She barely managed to pedal around to make enough deliveries to keep a roof over her head. She really ought to look for a new position, something exciting enough to jump-start her out of this peculiar lethargy. It was time to move on, but she simply didn't have the energy for a job search right now.

As April checked the first address on the list the dispatcher had given her, another cyclist shot down the hill leading to XPress Messenger Service. April squinted at the rider. Was it another courier or just a recreational biker?

She grinned. Definitely recreational and probably a novice at that, because every single item of his gear from his shiny, aerodynamic helmet to his fat, knobby tires was state-of-the-art and brand-spanking new without a scuff or a ding in sight.

She prepared to mount her own dilapidated Cannondale, glad at least that it had been recovered from its ordeal on the island, then stiffened. The helmet and wrap-around sunglasses disguised the face, but that body was devastatingly familiar.

Tyler pulled up beside her and dismounted awkwardly. "Hi," he said cheerfully.

April's jaw dangled somewhere around her knees. She would have been more inclined to accept a performing bear weaving through the downtown Seattle traffic than Tyler on a bike.

"What do you think of my new Trek?" he asked as proudly as a little boy on Christmas morning.

She looked at him more closely, then wished she hadn't. Her lower abdomen and environs tightened in an alarming way. As accustomed as she was to seeing them, she still thought men looked slightly comical in biking clothes, which was probably why most messengers were more apt to chose something like cutoff jeans or cargo shorts. But no one could say Tyler looked comical. Not in the slightest.

His black Lycra shorts hugged the most perfectly defined, muscular set of buns and thighs she'd ever seen and encased a truly magnificent bulge, which she quickly, guiltily looked away from, her face blazing with memories she had unsuccessfully tried to wipe away.

Unfortunately, her gaze skimmed up the rest of his body, and that sight also wasn't especially good at calming the rush of pure lust that was engulfing her. Tyler's tight, short-sleeved red racing jersey displayed his rock-hard biceps and broad shoulders and chest to perfection.

"What are you doing here, tricked out like that?" she asked rudely.

"Tsk, tsk, where are your manners, April? I admired your cycling skills and decided to take up the sport myself. Aren't you going to encourage me in my new interest?"

"Look, I don't know what you're up to, Nielsen, but it's not a sport to me. It's a business, and I've got work to do. So, if you'd just get out of my way..."

She leaped down hard on the pedals, crouched low over the handlebars and shot away from the sidewalk.

She watched the tiny image of Tyler in her rear-view mirror and chuckled at the surprised look on his face and the clumsy way he mounted his brand-new bike, but then the chuckle died in her throat, as he steadily gained on her with determined, powerful pedal strokes.

In no time at all he was breezing along beside her, and he didn't even sound winded.

"What I'm up to, April, is a chance to talk to you. Do you know how hard it was for me to see you all those weeks in court when you wouldn't say a word to me?"

"You didn't talk to me first." Rats! She sounded like a whiny grade-school kid.

She pulled ahead of him to pass a slow-moving truck and howled back over her shoulder, "Why did you ignore me at the hospital? Why wouldn't you return my calls after you got out?"

She ground her teeth together. *Oh, that was much better, definitely more grownup.* Now she sounded like a baby screaming for its mommy. She was regressing at an incredible rate. She simply couldn't keep the hurt and longing out of her voice.

He regained his place beside her. "I'm sorry. I was wrong. It's not easy for me to say this, but the truth is, I was... well, I was afraid."

"Afraid? Of me?"

"Of you and everything you remind me of that I'm not. At least that I haven't been. Spontaneous, light-hearted, willing to try new things, enjoying excitement—maybe even a thrill or two."

Without losing a beat, he zigzagged in tandem with her around a car door that opened right in front of them, when the driver didn't look to see if anyone was coming along behind her.

"I did a lot of soul-searching after I was released from the hospital," he continued, turning his head incautiously to the side to look at her. "It wasn't easy, thinking about my parents and my grandmother—and my own life. I've blocked that part of me for so long."

She didn't want to hear this, didn't want him confusing and upsetting her again, but her curiosity overcame her self-protective instincts. "So what did you figure out?"

"I believe I thought that if I just planned everything carefully enough I wouldn't get hurt anymore. I didn't want any surprises. I wanted to control everybody and everything around me to make sure my life ran smoothly, exactly the way I wanted it to. Then you came along." He grinned at her.

"Look out!" she warned. He was just about to ride right into a pothole the size of Lake Washington.

He zipped around it at the last second and rode next to her again, grin still in place. "You were one surprise right after another. I couldn't believe how attracted I was to you. I didn't want to be. I tried to deny it. Tried to kill it. I tried, but none of it worked."

"Right," she said sarcastically. "So, now you think I'm A-okay, is that it?" She tried to squash the little butterfly of hope that fluttered somewhere inside her.

"You guessed it. I didn't want to talk to you when I was in the hospital because I thought my heart would stop when you were up in that tree, getting ready to bash Smith in the head with the fishing pole. I was sure you were going to die, and there was nothing I could do about it. I blamed you for taking such a terrible chance. Then, after I'd been mad at you for about a month, almost hated you for causing me to be so afraid, finally, I realized you did exactly the right thing. There really wasn't anything else you could do. You came up with a course of action in only a few minutes that saved both of us. It wasn't foolhardy at all; it was brave and smart."

They stopped for a red light. Tyler pulled up close beside her. Now that he wasn't shouting to make her hear, his voice took on an earnestness and conviction that was hard to ignore.

"I don't want to be a stodgy, out-of-it nothing anymore. Someone who plots every day of his life right up to what coffin he'll be buried in without ever having any fun or excitement. I think you're the perfect woman to teach me how to become a little more quick-witted and how to enjoy myself."

April felt her insides coil into a pretzel. She wanted to believe him, but he wasn't the only one who was afraid. This wasn't like shooting the rapids in a kayak or facing down a belligerent trucker at an intersection. She didn't exactly enjoy being hurt herself.

"And what if I don't want to teach you?" she asked in a low voice.

He touched her shoulder and traced a path down her arm to her wrist. She restrained a gasp. His gentle touch incised her skin like a laser beam.

"Don't you care a little, April? You seemed to when we made love in the forest." His voice sounded ragged, raw. "It was the most powerful moment of my life."

April froze. How dare he mention their lovemaking when he'd heartlessly rejected her afterward? He was using a memory that was precious to manipulate her for some reason she didn't understand. She'd be crazy to think either of them could ever change enough to have a real relationship. She jerked her arm away from him.

"Well," he said, apparently trying for a lighter tone, "I care enough for both of us, and I'm a good student, too."

He patted the handlebars of his bike, as though it were a horse. "See, I'm already trying something new on my own even without a teacher's assignment."

April hooted. "Sure. A new bike does not make a character change, Tyler. It goes a lot deeper than that. You'd decide you didn't approve of me in no time at all."

The light changed to green. She tore off ahead of him then quickly swerved to ride between the lanes. A little white lining in heavy traffic would get rid of him.

Determined to get away, she sought all the most dangerous shortcuts she knew through the city. She flew over loading docks and across bridges, through parking garages and down narrow alleys. Finally, panting, she hopped a curb and pulled up in a pocket-sized park to catch her breath.

She'd only managed a couple of deep breaths, before Tyler came spinning down the street, leaped the curb and dropped his bike in the grass. He grasped both her arms.

"Don't you understand, April?" he rasped. "You can't make me give up. I love you, and I'm not going to let you get away."

April's head whirled. For the first time in her life, she thought she might faint. Love! Tyler loved her.

"But, Tyler," she stammered, "people don't change. I... I love you, too, but it would never work. We're too different. I've done a lot of thinking about us, too. You were always right about me; I don't stick with anything very long. As soon as I master one thing, I want to try something else."

Tyler threw back his head and laughed. "Well, I guess I'll just have to see to it that you never manage to master me."

He released her arms. Tenderly, he unfastened her helmet and removed it and her sunglasses. He took off his own and tossed them all to the ground. He looked deep in her eyes.

"Don't you see? I don't have to change. I actually liked digging in deep and using my wits to outsmart those crooks on the islands. It was thrilling! I'd never felt so alive before. And deep down I don't like to do the same things over and over again either. I've never put up cookie-cutter buildings. All of my architectural projects are different."

He kissed the very tip of her nose. The kiss tickled and burned and sparkled and made it very hard to think.

"I must have inherited something from my parents, after all. I'm really a lot like you; I've just buried it for years. We'll be great together. We've already put Smith and Willis and Harmon away where they belong, who knows what we might do in the future?"

He sneaked the kisses down an inch or so and found her mouth. "Who knows?" she echoed against his lips.

He pulled away and whooped joyfully. "I'll take that as a 'yes'!"

"A 'yes' to what?" she asked, bewildered.

"Why, to marriage, of course. What do you think of a world cruise for a honeymoon? La Paz, Mali, Sri Lanka, Tasmania?"

"I don't know," she said teasingly, her heart bursting with happiness. "All those new places and people—uncertain transportation, weird money, diseases. Wouldn't that be dangerous?"

"Not if you take the right precautions. I'd plan it for you perfectly. Itineraries for every country and..."

She put her hands flat against his chest. "No itineraries," she said firmly.

He blinked, grinned sheepishly, then claimed her mouth again. "Oh, okay," he said between kisses. "I forgot for a minute. You might have to be patient with me occasionally. But I promise, a reminder will do the trick. No schedules. No itineraries."

April kissed him back with all her heart. Her mother had been right all along—marriage and family. The idea thrilled her. She was about to embark on the greatest adventure of her life, and it wasn't a world tour.

"No schedule," she whispered, "just love."

Meet

Linda Wallace

Linda Wallace grew up on a farm in Missouri, a glorious place for childhood. She spent the first seven or eight years of her life pretending to be a horse galloping and nickering in her yard and the surrounding fields. The nearest "city" a few miles from the farm is Arrow Rock with a grand total of 75 residents. But Arrow Rock is no ordinary country hamlet. The Arrow Rock Lyceum, an equity summer repertory theatre, brings glamour and fantasy to Missouri every summer. Ignoring the fact that her acting skills are negligible, Linda likes to say she's a "professional" actor, unlike most wannabe waiter/taxi driver/actors, because as a reward for long hours of babysitting for the theater's director during her high school years, she was given a paying role as Rose in *She Stoops to Conquer.*

Since her girlhood days, Linda has lived in many cities all across the U.S. from Kealakekua on the big island of Hawaii to the Bronx in New York. Her three children's births were spaced across the country, too; the oldest was born in New York, middle child in Kansas, and youngest in Hollywood. She currently lives in Seattle with her husband and cat, and yes, she loves the rain. Jobs and interests have been equally wide-ranging including nurses' aid, stockings clerk at Macy's in Manhattan, waitress at the Kailua-Kona Hilton, weekly newspaper publisher, advertising salesperson for *The Los Angeles Times,* elementary school para-educator, and administrative assistant. Everywhere she's gone, though, one of the first considerations was always where was the closest library. For underpinning all else is the love of books. Linda knew how important books were going to be in her life ever since she jumped off the little yellow bus returning her home from Arrow Rock's two-room school and ran up the country drive, shouting to her mother, "I can read, I can read!"

Get in touch with Linda at:

Home Page: www.linda-wallace.com
E-mail Address: contact@linda-wallace.com